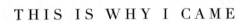

THIS IS WHY I CAME

THIS IS
WHY I
CAME

A NOVEL

MARY RAKOW

COUNTERPOINT
BERKELEY

Library of Congress Cataloging-in-Publication Data

Rakow, Mary.
This is why I came : a novel / Mary Rakow.
    pages ; cm
ISBN 978-1-61902-575-2 (hardcover)
1. Women authors—Fiction. I. Title.

PS3618.A44T48 2015
813'.6--dc23

                            2015009415

ISBN 978-1-61902-575-2

Cover design by Kelly Winton
Interior design by meganjonesdesign.com

COUNTERPOINT
2560 Ninth Street, Suite 318
Berkeley, CA 94710
www.counterpointpress.com

Printed in the United States of America
Distributed by Publishers Group West

10 9 8 7 6 5 4 3 2 1

In 1955 at Ronchamp Le Corbusier said, "Certain things are sacred and others are not, regardless of whether or not they are religious." To describe the space he'd built there he used the phrase, "Ineffable space." "Ineffable," the un-understandable.

S HE HAS COME after an absence of many years. The cab was late, she is angry and her neck hurts, up the back, over the top of her head, so that she tries to remember not to rub it as she sits on her chair in a row with others. She doesn't want to be angry at the cab driver, doesn't want to worry that her headaches could mean a tumor or cancer. Doesn't want to be afraid of aging and death, always afraid and worrying. She knows it isn't just age. When she was young she was also a believer and she rode through her life feeling held from behind and below as if in a rickshaw, calm and still as she moved without fear into her future. She knows that her faith gave her those things, cheerfulness, generosity, detachment, faith strong enough to cast out fear. But she can't find her way back.

IT IS GOOD FRIDAY afternoon, the Passion has been reenacted by the school children and the church is dark, quiet and cool. The statues have been draped in purple all of Lent, and now, in addition, a further stripping away, the flowers have also been removed from the altar and the three layers of white linen reverently folded by the young altar servers, so that the altar is bare, just wood, which she finds almost embarrassing in its nakedness.

She had forgotten that people see each other in line, see each other come out of the confessional, some crying, some not, some inside a long time, others briefly. Waiting is both public and deeply private. Two teenage boys stand, letting older men and women like herself have their chairs. The first boy goes in, comes out, moves silently to a pew and kneels, lost in his thoughts. She moves a chair closer. In the half-darkness a simple candle casts a warm light on the confessional's narrow door.

On the floor, at an angle against the shallow steps that lead to the altar, a wood cross larger than life rests and on it the corpus. One by one, people kneel down, touch it in their different ways, a hand lingering, another stroking, an embrace, a kiss. One woman shows her young child, a baby girl just learning to walk, to be quiet and still, to wait.

IT IS HARD to keep awake, her body folded over on the chair, hard because it is all more beautiful than she remembers and the beauty weighs down on her like a heavy cape. Hard because the strangers are welcoming in their reserve, hard because she feels all that she has missed, time folded over and onto itself like a paper bird with pert wings, those sharp folds of something flat into something that could fly, the Holy Spirit like a dove, all of it pressing down with awe and sorrow, sorrow being time's twin.

After an absence of more than thirty years, she's at last come back inside the walls, into the body of the whale, and it is more beautiful because it is more real to her than she expected, that is the trouble, and that is why she is staying, why she has taken the little hand-made book out of her purse and fingers its rough edges while her eyes are closed, feels the tiny white stitches where she sewed the center seam, the uneven bulkiness because on some pages she also taped images cut from magazines, art museum catalogues, photocopies from art books in her home because the images spoke to her of what she had written in various inks over the years, blue, black, green, making a Bible of her own, a testament where she could cast a thread through the silence and separation and anger of those years, some line to catch herself, strong enough to bear her full weight, dragging her through the water, the hook still caught in the side of her cheek, the cheek flesh healed around it, the wounds of Christ, lying, as he is now, on the incline of the shallow steps leading to the altar, his long carved legs bent at the knee, the nail driven through the arches of his feet, one stacked on the other like kindling, that ancient way of seeing him, timeless, that ancient way of saying, "Suffering is why I came, Bernadette."

Maybe she will show the priest her book. See where my needle carried the thread? See this picture of Adam I taped in? See this image of Mary Magdalen, so sorrowful with her jar of oil?

Her little book with its tidy Table of Contents. She has come because she somehow wants to join the book to the corpus on the floor, the faithful moving slowly up the aisle to reverence it, the wood and paint and real people, real pews, real altar, that place of radical change, real nails that were hammered into real flesh centuries ago, all of it, ancient and visceral, weaving and interweaving of past and present, waking and dream, to make of all of it, if that joining is possible, one thing, one glorious, true thing.

Eyes still closed, she feels the cool pages for the image of Adam, the first. To the artist, it wasn't Adam, but to her it became the image of the one she calls, "the Maker."

Slumping on her chair, the line long, she dreams each story again as if it were new.

TABLE OF CONTENTS

I.

II.

I.

1

Adam the Maker

E FASHIONS PEACOCK, dove, and parakeet, all the species
and subspecies, microscopic and immense, yet is unable, no
matter how hard he tries, to make the form he longs to see, the
song he hears but cannot put outside himself, unable to compose
the right sequence of notes, unable to make the form that will tell
him who he *is*.

He traces his hand, his foot, in the sand. Lying on his back,
reaches over his chest with a stick, traces his entire body there then
stands, but it does not move, unable to make a form like himself
that also *breathes*. The water erasing it like an encouraging teacher
at first, saying, try, try again, then mocking.

Destroying this drawing and that. All around the island, in
the wet sand and dry, sketches and more sketches, pages in messy
piles under the trees, floating on the lakes, clay models on the
riverbanks, countless mud statues, all of them false. Fabricated
then abandoned, revised, fabricated anew then abandoned again.
Clumsy or elegant, it doesn't matter. The debris is everywhere and

the animals are multiplying faster than he can keep up, all of it not what he wants to see.

He cannot find a way to put out into the world the form he cannot *not* see. Bound by this need more visceral than if his legs were bound by leather straps tight on his body, digging in. If he walks to the left it is there. If he walks to the right it is with him. This formless thing demanding a form and he cannot get it right. Draft after draft after draft.

"We had such high expectations for you!" he hears the waves say. Sometimes he thinks it is the chorus of animals, donkeys and macaws, jealous that he is not satisfied with them. "Why are you despondent?" the robin asks, "Look at my wings!" and the ant, "Look at my diligence!" And he does look, trying to preserve what is left of hope, and does study his companions that are his successes and so near, but this does not solve the problem and brings no peace.

Out of respect, he has given all of them their individual names, zebra, koi, antelope. But the real name for each, the name he keeps to himself, is "Not-me." You are Not-me. You also are Not-me. It is endless, the diversity of what is Not-me a torment, so that finally at one sunset at the close of one particular day, the remnant of hope impossible to revive, he denies his desire, denies whatever it is that pushes him to transcend who he is, to exceed all the animals and the plants and the stars, the sea and the dry land, all that he has already made, even though it is all, and he knows this, which is a mystery and confusing, that it is all undeniably good.

He imagines, instead, the pleasure of not being driven, and so formulates a different end to his loneliness and, taking the sharp blade, lies down thinking to end his life. It seems dignified. A gate to relief, perhaps even to happiness. But when he lifts the blade over his abdomen he fails again, unable to pierce himself, as if failure were endless, as if failure itself is what he is best at inventing, and finding that he lacks the necessary courage falls asleep hoping to never wake.

SHE COMES TO him in a dream so startling it wakes him and he sees that she is not a dream at all but is as real as the field mouse, the ostrich, the hen and hawk. For a long time they stare at each other without speech, motion, and he compares her to the elegance of the serpent and imagines her softness like the goose's down. Seeing that she is unlike the other creatures he has made, he thinks her name will not be Not-me but perhaps Not Not-me, yet seeing that she is equal to himself, does not name her at all but asks, "What is your name?" and she replies "Eve."

He wonders from where she comes. Wonders, since he has not made her, if there is a maker mightier than himself, one who, by implication, holds him in a deep understanding, his hunger clearly and intimately known by this other, as it has now been made visible in its answer, which causes him, as he stares at her, arm and leg and neck, to wonder if all the creatures in the sea and on the dry land and all the stars in the heavens that he thought he had made weren't made by him at all, but rather by this other. And he desires to know this one, and names the maker he cannot see but whose work he sees, "God."

2

Cain and Abel

A BEL, AN INVALID, in the covering of night, took aim and threw the stone out the window, hitting the ewe. He dragged himself outside, everyone asleep, and thought, this time I will not ask Cain to hide what I have done from our father. Instead Abel slit the ewe's throat, watched the blood drain onto the grass and slowly, with great difficulty, gathered wood, lit a fire, and waited, hoping, rather than fearing his father, to please him.

In the morning Cain arrived bringing poppy cakes, breads and crackers, flaxseed, cooked squash and onions. He loved his work, setting down the seeds, vines grafted, the grapes better each year, the sweet fruits handled gently, packed in boxes with straw. He'd prepared lentils with mint, parsley and olive oil, his father's favorite. But when his mother opened the door Cain saw his father already at the table, a bone in his hand, pulling flesh with his teeth, oil dripping from his fingers, the flesh still pink, the fat crispy. "We'll have those later," he pointed to Cain's fruits and grains, waving him in, but Cain stood at the door terrified, then fled.

BLOOD STAINED THE ground where the young ewe was slain. Weeping, Cain gathered what remained, recognized its soft hide, its four dainty hooves, its head with two ears flush with stiff hair, that it was the new one, the youngest, the one they hadn't yet named. He wept for the ewe until anger rose up his back like heat and when he stood he knew that he could not *not* harm his brother. That vengeance would come to Abel, and come through him.

To others Abel was known as the weak brother, tender-hearted, the poor invalid, but to Cain, Abel was the one who threw stones at his sheep, lambs and baby goats, the one who found pleasure that way, wounding them so they could no longer run like the wind but would be broken like he was. Sometimes Abel taunted Cain, taking aim at the first born saying, "He's like you!" because Cain was the first born, and continued until Cain cried out, "Stop!"

Like fire on dry grass, the news spread and in a short time Abel had assistants, a new livelihood. Animals, no longer given family names, were raised to be slaughtered. Cows, goats, chickens, even the turtledoves. Old words changed their meaning. "Tender" no longer meant an animal's sweet disposition but how its flesh slid between the teeth. "Tough" no longer fierce and noble like the bull, but a lack of fat and undesirable. Animals became "meat," their bodies cut into parts and each part also named, "flank steak," "rump roast," and "ribs." Abel taught others how to slaughter mercifully and Cain thought, he's teaching as if he'd been merciful. My brother a hero. "How did you discover this?" they asked him. "Even my crops are thriving!" "My daughter walks again!" And Cain wondered, is he growing in compassion while I grow in bitterness?

Cain grieved that animals were slain, and always would be slain. He neglected his fields, grapes on his vines withered, then the vines themselves fell. It seemed that blood was everywhere—on tabletops, in bowls, smeared on aprons so that he could no longer bring himself to eat red foods, pomegranate, watermelon, kidney bean. His mother's consolations fell away like water, making him feel more alone, while his father, jovial and proud of Abel, so long an embarrassment to him, made jokes about the new foods. Eating the calf's heart, its liver and brains, said, "Surely this is sweet bread!" which stung Cain, his raisin breads and fruit tarts, his barley and dates. "It's just a joke!" his father said, touching the back of Cain's head, squeezing his neck for emphasis.

Cain left messages, wanting to be remembered by his family. Nut cakes and fruit spreads in jars tied with string. "Look under the table," and, "It's in the garden, love, Cain." But they did not look. He told himself, I would have looked. I would have read notes from my son.

EVERYONE SEEMED TO be doing passionate things. A tightrope walker tied his rope between trees and danced across it like a bird. A man lying on the grass held a heavy woman to himself, her thighs like barrels, lost in pleasure, the grass sticking to her legs. A girl in a sleeveless top with shapely arms played a flute for three of her friends. Life had taken a wonderful turn. But when Cain approached a bench to sit down, the women covered their heads with scarves and he thought, they're pretending to hide their faces from the sun but really they're hiding from me. A bell tolled two o'clock then three. He watched shoes, the bottoms of legs, sandals, bare feet, ankle bells, toe rings, his eyes most comfortable looking down. A man walked past wearing a skirt flounced out by a petticoat. A print of thrones and, at his sleeves, ruffles. Cain had never seen such a silhouette and it pleased him, but then he thought, I've never dressed like that. I have never been original.

He felt inferior to Abel and to anything on which his eye fell. The rabbit is softer than I am to touch. The owl more wise. The raven more bold. The snake more elegant in the moon's blue light.

In the new world filled with enterprises and projects, memory called to Cain of the life he used to live, held in a cycle of planting and harvest, of bare vines that sprung new leaves and grapes year after year, leaving for a time then re-appearing. Memory called with tiny bells and sweet songs so that Cain tasted it like honey on his lips and tongue, then the back of his tongue, so sweet his teeth ached and, again, his anger grew fierce against his brother.

IT WAS EASY. Abel was sleeping when Cain carried him to the spot where the first ewe was slain and, lifting a large stone, threw it down on Abel. And when it was over, Cain felt relief, Abel lying there.

He waited for Abel's eyes to open, to return like the grape and the wheat, but Abel's eyes did not open. He watched his brother's blood seep into the dirt so that the earth became soft like a full sponge and still Abel remained as he lay.

CAIN LIFTED ABEL and ran with him to the fields that once were his and made a bed of the dry vines and lay down cradling his brother saying, "You will rise up like the wheat that comes and is gone and then comes again." But Abel did not rise up. Cain watched Abel's skin turn blue then white then grey and stroked the cold flesh of his brother as it stiffened. Then horrified, thought, what have I done?

DAY AFTER DAY, Cain lay with his brother on the vine heap, covering him with his body, fighting off vultures, flies, but Abel did not stir. And Cain wept for his brother because he saw that Abel was not like the wheat and the grape and the barley but was like the ewe after all. And he repented for what he had done and wept and wondered, will this come to everyone? And Cain named what had happened to Abel, "Death."

BUT ON THE seventh day, through the dry stalks, through the stiff, putrid body of his brother, came a voice like the voice of the earth saying, "Come, find me, Cain! Come find me!" and it was Abel when they were young, playing in the tall rows of corn, before the accident, when Abel could run like the cheetah. Abel's voice was alive and real and Cain thought, my brother is neither like the wheat that comes back nor the ewe that is slain. And he considered Abel and thought, perhaps we are all like this, neither wheat nor ewe. And Cain called Abel and himself and his family and neighbors, "Human."

3

Cain and the Dream
of the City

CAIN DREAMT OF a city and the dream grew around him like comfort. Alabaster staircases with graceful, shallow steps, tall white buildings like layered cakes, boulevards, lanterns, ballrooms, music halls, museums, a scriptorium with a gold-tiled vestibule, precise instruments, a fencing school, astronomy, tradesmen, mask-making shops, a jester, a harlequin, ivory beds, combs, pins and spoons. Irrigation canals, coats of arms, gymnasts competing in parks. He dreamt of diverse nomenclatures, sciences, precise theories of color, laws of motion. He would have a tea shop and serve cool drinks garnished with colorful paper umbrellas, honeydew and mint. He wanted smooth surfaces, glossy and promising, clarity, simplicity, the manufacture of elegant things, accouterments, precious objects with fine joints. Nothing with blood in it. Nothing with breath.

In the sumptuousness of the city, draftsmen and masons would build towers that reached Heaven. He would climb them with ease and would be able to speak to God that way. And God would say, "Cain, leave your sorrow and guilt here with me." And he would at last be free of the burden he carried for the death of his brother.

SO CAIN LEFT the land of his family and journeyed east, toward the sun.

BUT GOD CAME to Cain in a dream saying, "If you build towers to Heaven you will be like us." And Cain woke from the dream and did not build his city with its towers and porticos, did not procure the skills of artisans and chefs, because he saw in God the jealousy that had poisoned his own heart and the heart of his brother.

Instead, he rose from his bed and, using the skills he already possessed, employing no one, made a garden. He fenced off the land and filled the enclosure with gravel, which would never die, and in this way he occupied himself, raking his garden year after year, making a small, elegant world without wheat or olive trees, blood or breath.

BUT ONE DAY, in this quiet activity, the future came vividly toward him.

He saw a city with canals and small islands and slim boats manned by men wearing striped shirts. Engineers had built homes, museums, restaurants, and some strong beautiful buildings with bell towers that reached to the clouds.

Inside were statues and paintings. In the damp climate painters learned that plaster did not set well so they shifted to canvas and wood. Cain saw one painting titled, "Cain Killing Abel" and cried as he raked because he did not recognize himself or his brother there and felt again the gap between himself and the world. The year was 1544 and people were dying in great numbers. The painter also died of the great plague and Cain noticed his tomb in a building called Iglesia de Santa Maria Gloriosa dei Frari.

He saw that, though towers were built, men and women did not climb them to talk to God but entered Santa Maria Gloriosa and other such buildings to lay their burdens down without climbing at all. He watched them go in and come out. Many seemed changed, as if possessing what he himself longed for. To feel light again, innocent and at peace. He called what people seemed to find in those buildings, "Forgiveness." And he named the places where they seemed to find it, "Church," "Temple," "Synagogue," and "Mosque."

WHEN THE VISION lifted and Cain was again alone with his gravel and rake, he felt how much he wanted to live in such a city, but he could no more transport himself into that future than he could into the deep past before Abel's injury, when they were in the sweet field.

He found himself held in the sound of the gravel parting as he drew the fingers of the rake slowly through it and surrendered to the sound, his body heavy with the death of his brother. But then Cain heard a soft song coming from a land of ice and snow and blue light. A chieftain was dying and words came to him, which he sang, and the words then came to Cain as he raked more slowly still, setting the end of the rake in the groove he'd just made, all parallel, ordered, all bloodless and clean. The words of the snow king came into Cain's garden and settled onto the gravel and then settled into Cain's heart.

> *Hear me, smith of the heavens,*
> *And heal me.*
>
> *Drive out,*
> *O king of suns,*
>
> *Every human sorrow*
> *From the city of my heart.*

4

Noah

EVERYTHING HAD ASTONISHED God. Making all of creation *de novo*, from nothing. He even liked the sound of it, murmuring "de novo" to himself.

He first created nothingness, a deep blue robe, and covered himself with it, his neck and thighs, down to his ankles, then the sky and the stars, over 243 species of turtles alone. And last, to see himself more clearly, he created man, male and female, all of his intimacies, his genitals, torso, his breasts and thighs, to never die. Seeing that it was good, God espoused himself to it like a young groom, binding himself as with a vow, to love his espoused forever. Exuberant, he gave his bride every herb bearing seed, every beast, every fish and fowl and crawling thing, dominion over all he had made as a wedding gift, a dowry.

BUT WHEN THEY multiplied on the earth, instead of love, like himself, he saw wickedness and it grieved God. He had trouble seeing himself in the breeze, in the pony's hide, in the daffodil and most of all in man, where the heart was so powerful for ill. It afflicted God, recalling that wedding union, that shower of rice. The more he paced and searched, the more he could not find himself, not in man and not in the mountain or glacier, the forest or the rivers, so that in time he recoiled at the thought of looking, and came to hate what once was magnificent, and to hate himself for making it and espousing himself to it.

He dreamt of drowning with his own hands everything in the sea and on the dry land. Giraffe and lemur, every hive of bees, every plant that pollinates, every fruit in decay, every bird in flight, every mammal suckling its young. And when he considered man, his anger was unstoppable. "You always want one more thing. But I don't have one more thing! There's just me. If I gave you myself, you'd find fault with me, too." He imagined drowning all that belonged to man alone, every embrace and dream, every memory, every idea and regret, every instance of laughter and relief. And God calmed himself this way, soothed by the violence of it, the erotic charge of destruction.

NOAH FELT THE anger of God and waited to see what he already sensed. A great wind came and bent the trees to the ground, snapping them, then the night sky bright with lightning, the stars disappeared. "All this might be severed," he said to his wife as he looked at the sky, sheltering his eyes. In the bellowing cattle, he heard the anger of God. In his neighbor's argument. For many nights he was frightened and could not sleep. "The minute God stops forgiving us," he told his daughters and sons, "all of this," he gestured in an arc, "will come to an end."

He beckoned God but heard nothing. He lost his appetite, his sense of direction. His wife, hanging out clothes, watched him and remembered what she'd seen when they first met, that he was unlike other men, a visionary, his eyes full of a future. He spoke of what they could make together, a shared life. It was what she most loved in him, so that she said, "Make it of gopher wood," because sometimes her suggestions brought him back to himself, and it did. Noah rose and paced, marked out measurements in the yard, drove in stakes with white flags, three hundred cubits by fifty, and determination returned to his face. He raced and hammered, outgrowing one ladder then the next, his teeth grinding as he slept, never fast enough. He ordered his sons to gather all that was beautiful on the earth, kumquat and alligator, hen, lizard and magpie.

WHEN HER SONS were gone weeks then months, leaving behind wives and small children, the wives becoming despondent, frantic, then despondent again, her grandchildren forgetting the names of their fathers, Noah's wife grew bitter. As he hammered, Noah wept for all he could see, animals, neighbors, bushes and trees so that she wondered how thin the line was between vision and madness.

When his sons returned, seeing the assembly, he wept again, for all that was strange and lovely, leopard, hyena and whippoorwill. Ferocious animals collared and tied to stakes, makeshift cages held in place by ropes. Bulbs and ferns gathered in boxes, and saplings.

Some of the pairs already mating, neighbors protested the noise, smell, and commotion. Some moved away. The sound of hammering was constant, the awkward vessel casting its enormous shadow over the garden and the house so that she had trouble keeping hold of her affection for Noah, and thought, if this continues, he will strip everything I care about away.

WHEN THE FIRST raindrops jangled the wind chime outside their bedroom window, Noah woke and pulled open the blind, sickened. Grey drops, a mist, hovered over the fields, the horses pawed the ground. Again, he called out to God but heard nothing so ordered his sons to lead the animals in two by two. His wife walked apart, not with him, up the ramp, hoping, in the noise and confusion, he wouldn't notice.

THE LOWLY GRASS was the first to disappear, the cats and mice floated on the streams between houses. A dog swam in the current, a chest of drawers. Noah's daughters shielded the eyes of their children, ordered them away from the windows, their friends and playmates frantically swimming then screaming then going under. Rocks and boulders, fences, rooftops, people on the roofs screaming, people in trees leaping to the ark, the thud of their bodies and others leaping to their deaths. The water rose and the ark rose until just the uppermost leaves of the trees were visible, the giant hawks waging war against it. The footpaths on the hills disappeared then the tops of the hills and then the water crept up the mountainsides, the goats stampeded straight up, leaping across rocks and ridges, terrified. Noah thought, surely God's holy mountain will not disappear, but then it did, and there was nothing left to see but water and sky and Noah thought, God has brought the waters of the flood over his head like a cloak.

WHEN THE DOG floated by, Noah said to himself, love is stronger than this. And he clung to that one sentence as to a plank floating on the water, a single plank, repeating it to himself again and again.

As whitecaps formed on the water, slamming into the ark from all sides, the giant swells, the sea creatures, great whales calling their distress, "This is how much God loved us," Noah told himself, losing balance, grabbing the ledge. Somehow a birdcage bobbed upright before going under, the parakeet frantic on the swing.

DAYS PASSED, WEEKS. Noah rationed the food more strictly, put the animals on half-stock, the grain for mules. Afloat, isolated, Noah's wife saying, "What made you think we were a seafaring family?" The children had nightmares, months became a year then two until, finally, the children forgot what they'd seen and composed new rhymes and games and hand-slaps, the girls jumped rope to the sound of it. Horses, goats, sheep gave birth, the stillborn thrown into the sea. Wives grew hungry for new touch, experimented, comingled.

Fighting, grumbling, the ark became a floating prison without destination or purpose. "You brought us here just to die!" his wife accused. One dead child already thrown overboard. Animals restless to fly, to run. The children's legs shrunk, their arms grew crooked, their vocabularies became crude. They spoke to each other in guttural sounds and Noah turned away thinking, this is the death of language.

He wanted to touch his wife but she withdrew, so he slept in the storeroom, the key around his neck. Tied himself to the shelf now empty, where grain had stood in bags and made his bed there, the smell of pitch near his face. He bumped against the inside wall of the ark, rubbing against it like fire, combustible, while the anger of God slammed the side of the vessel again and again without cease, the slamming waves then thunder.

When his wife banged at the door complaining of cow dung and shortage, ants, the multiplying rats, he ignored her, tied the straps tighter, binding himself to the anger of God whom he also cursed for drawing him into life in the first place, for making the moon and the stars, for making his wife, so beautiful when she was young, the trees that sung when he walked her home. He cursed God for the primrose, the flesh of the date, the smell of crisp meat, loganberries and wine, the shade of the pines, so that his body, his senses, flailed at the memory of it. Most vehemently he cursed God himself whom he once loved more than his wife, his family, his flocks and fields.

He recalled the night his good neighbor stood at the door saying, "It was a mercy killing," and handed Noah the pillow he'd put over his wife. He relayed how he'd sat at the edge of the bed telling her a story from his childhood, a happy story that made her mouth smile, the side that still moved, then reached for the pillow and pressed it to her face. "A large pillow," he emphasized, asking Noah to burn it for him. Large enough to cover not just her face but her chest, shoulder to shoulder, so that nothing was left to chance.

Some nights Noah wondered if he should have done the same thing. His wife and family senseless on the water, the life they had, obliterated, their future would be what? To throw each other overboard when it was time?

He practiced telling himself, this is not the absence of love but love broken, love is stronger than death, love perdures. Telling himself this when his oldest son knocked reverently but firmly on the door saying, "Father, come out. Mother died last night and we need you. We're throwing her into the sea."

NOAH LOOSED THE straps and unlocked the door and saw that his grandchildren were adults, his own body too frail to walk unassisted, his wife's hair grown down to her feet. They took off her wedding ring and gave it to him, then wrapped her in a linen cloth, and, lifting her body over the rail, let her go.

As he watched her body disappear, he put the ring to his lips and tongue to taste her salt there and recalled how his wife had for many nights beseeched him to come out but he'd refused, and when, through the door, she asked his forgiveness he withheld it from her. He had needed her to be with him when they walked up the ramp, had needed her all of the time, and when she lingered behind, shuffling in the rabbits and butterflies, he told himself, this is the beginning of the end.

Unforgiven, she'd passed years carrying a candle behind her cupped hand, speaking to him through the door saying, "Come back to our marriage bed, please come back to me." But he did not unlock the door. In their bed alone, she'd imagined her husband returning to her, to the little rope-strung bed he'd made for them, the maroon blanket, the flickering lamp, their arms around each other, speaking soft words with tenderness. "We were a couple, we were a pair," she would remind him, rubbing the red marks on his ankles and wrists where he'd bound himself to the shelf, his bruises, splinters in his back and on his feet. He would watch her pluck them out, her hair grown coarse, not as soft to the touch. He would notice this and she his haggard face. They would lie side by side, her back inches from his face, the mole near her backbone, between her shoulder blades, the sag of her skin. "We're still alive," he would remind her. "And we have each other," she would add, bringing his wrinkled hand over her shoulder to her breast.

In that moment, ring to his lips, the endless sea before him, Noah saw God abscond down a marble corridor without end, his blue robe flapping at his heels. He watched God walk away until he came to an empty throne, seraphim and cherubim carved in linden wood, plated in gold, and instead of seeing him mount the throne he watched God crouch behind it, hidden.

IT FRIGHTENED NOAH. The rocking stopped and a great silence swept through the ark. The animals, silent, the children in their play.

In time, the waters shrank and the dry land appeared. His sons opened the door, released the animals and the children, grandchildren and great-grandchildren, while Noah stayed in the empty ark. The Almighty has exhausted himself, that is all, Noah thought. He doesn't even want his anger anymore.

He rummaged for berries on the floor, the abandoned pot long cold, the barley and lentils rotten, the tallow gone from the lamps. He would stay in the ark until he at least felt grateful that there was a limit to God's anger, no matter how long that took.

HE SAW THE white hall without end, God crouching there year after year, without majesty, emptied, only the sound of his own breathing, magnified, the inhalation and exhalation falling off the walls, echoing without interruption. He saw the throne sprinkled with blood, the blood of all the animals and children and men and women who had been drowned, and those who had died and were thrown overboard, his wife. And so Noah rose, shut the storage room door, descended the ramp, and slowly gathered stones. He lit a fire and watched the smoke rise as it always had in the world he had known. He called his children, grandchildren and great-grandchildren, all dispersed, taking the llama and parrot, the salamander in its shallow dish, and they came. In the white hall, the throne sprinkled with blood, he could smell it, he could hear the breathing of God, slow and deathlike, and Noah spoke the new word in a language he did not know. "Hilasterion" he said to the sand and the worn hem of his robe. And Noah pitied God and came to love his fragility because he was like man. "Mercy Seat," he said again, place of propitiation.

AND GOD HEARD the word, thinking it a dream, and opened his eyes.

TO HIS CHILDREN and their families, a great gathering, Noah said, "There are times when even the marriage vows cannot be kept. Times when extraordinary conditions make it impossible." The small children were quiet, so he continued. "Your mother and I deserted each other," he looked at his daughters and sons. "But God is merciful."

When Noah spoke these last words mercy itself made its way into the ear of God and quickened him. Noah continued. "The holiness of God is boundless and his love is without limit. So we must forgive ourselves and start again, here. For God's love is greater than any form in which it dwells."

IN THE WHITE glistening hall without end, God heard Noah and stood, remembering himself and his power. He smoothed his hair and remembered that he alone was the source of all holiness. He felt the fullness of his royal power and draped himself again in the imperial robes, his embroidered cope, and stood on the exuberant foliate pattern that appeared on the rug, gold armlets on the sleeves of his tunic, his chest lavishly decorated with strings of pearls. "I will espouse myself again," God said and put on the palladium of the defender of the walls. He walked toward the opening of the hallway full stride then ran, pearls banging against his chest, taking with him the new gift he created for his betrothed and, breathless, he stepped, magnificent and noble, out of the palace of memory.

NOAH LOOKED UP to the holy mountain and, seeing a great nimbus of light, fell to the ground and the congregation with him. Something on the surface under his fingertips was changing. He turned his head. The same was happening to the hills and the sky.

Trembling, he asked God, "What is this?"

"I made it for you."

"But what do you call it? It is everywhere and so beautiful!"

And God said, "Color."

WHEN GOD ASKED Noah to name the colors, he protested, "I'm not good with words. My wife was the one."

But God said, "Please. Do it for me."

Looking at the nearby tree, the smooth fruit as it was changing, the leaves one color, the trunk another, the branches and the birds, each its own, Noah thought of his wife's smooth hair when she was young, that it would have been the same color as the smooth fruit of the tree, so he called it, "chestnut."

"YOU CAME BACK," Noah said.

And God answered, "You made me anew."

THEN NOAH NAMED the different bands of color around the face of God an "Arc" and called them "red," "orange," "yellow," "green," "blue" and "indigo." The last he called "violet" and told God, "This will be your color. The color of penance and royalty."

5

Abraham and Isaac

EACH STEP ACROSS the sand, for the seven days they walked, Abraham rehearsed the history of his holiness. I gave You not only my lambs without blemish and my new calf but also my ripest fruit. . . .

It all came back to him as he walked. Isaac ahead, bound by ropes at his wrists, weights on his ankles, the two soldiers accompanying them on horseback.

He liked having an audience, liked walking and making his son walk, the humility of it. Isaac wearing the same scarf around his mouth, the black one reserved for this purpose. It was a glorious sight to Abraham, sparkling and vivid.

THE SOLDIERS LAY Isaac on the pile of stones and retreated as they had each time. Abraham already aroused by the sight of his son, bound and helpless, the little twigs.

COVER ME WITH your sweetness, Isaac! Your child's body without hair. Your legs like peaches. Give me your skin, let me pull it over my head and shoulders like a cape. Your foreskin over me, that I might go into the tent of your body. You smell of powder. I have to strike the match, don't you see? Your ankles quivering but I am covered with shame, Isaac. Bathe me with your blood. Bring the song of salvation back to my lips.

YOUR ASHES ON my forehead, your ashes on my beard.

6

Isaac Afterward

O R MAYBE ABRAHAM did not kill Isaac.

SO THAT AFTERWARD Isaac had nightmares that became dreams in daytime, no longer requiring darkness but stood firm against sunlight, that real.

WHEN HIS SOFT peach hair grew coarse and curly over his body, the dreams became one dream recurring, all the parts taken into himself, the flame carried seven days, the ascent, the stones against his back, the ropes, his father above him, the flame that singed his forearms before it was withdrawn.

"TAKE ME," he begs in his dream, the other bringing silk ties from a closet, binding Isaac's ankles and wrists. Mind binding the body, the body bound so that the mind, immobile, relieved at last, rests. Across the sheet, the pillow cases, a sliding door. In such a room, on such a bed, in just those moments, unable to move, he pleads, make flight impossible. Even the notion of flight. "Tie hard," he says. The frantic bird, panicked, bats its wings, escapes the bush into air and then is shot down, the dog pointing, its paw cocked, its tail straight out, let that not be me. Bind me to this ground. Press hard, your body on mine, until it registers as pain. Take me to that edge where death waits, flammable. Hold me there until love seems again possible, until I surrender to it, facile, untarnished, O sweet liberty.

7

Sarah and Abraham

O NCE HOME, FEELING the weight of a deed he could not remember, he asked the soldiers why they were mounted, why the fancy saddles, why was there blood on everything he touched? He heard the stones cry out. The black scarf.

He demanded Sarah replace the bedding, the drape, again and again, the plates. Awake many nights in a row, wildly gesturing, saying of the bedroom, the garden, the hills, "This is all illusion! Now I have clarity! Now I am really myself!" Adrift in the moonlight then collapsing to bed, asleep for days and then for weeks, eating nothing but broth, crying at small things that didn't usually make him cry, saying, also with tears, that he loved her, that he was not a great man, pacing as if the whole project of the world were in his head like a problem to be solved.

WHEN HE TOOK their first child and returned alone, Sarah wanted her child back but not her husband. Each time, again and again, she loved him less, then despised him, then hated.

With each child, she took the clothing, blankets and toys and buried them along with the knife, waiting for her husband to be himself again, for him to rise clear-eyed, to wash and ask pleasantly, "Where is Zachary?" or, "Where is Nathan?" or, "Where is Deborah, I haven't seen her all day?"

"You've had a dream," she'd learned to say. "We had no such child."

BUT THIS TIME, on this day, in her old age, Isaac, whose skin smelled like honey, Isaac who would be her last, the soldiers mounted and waiting, the scarf taken from the drawer, she said to Abraham, "I accuse you!" and then, "I accuse us." And she recited the name of each child he had slain. "You, Abraham of the Chaldees."

He was packing his knapsack and stopped. Eyes wide with fury, he raised his arm against her but she stood firm, saying, "Return with Isaac or you will live alone forever."

8

Isaac in the Field

"TELL ME ABOUT them," Isaac said when Sarah revealed that he was not the first child born but was the first to survive and took him to the place marked off by a fence where flowers grew inside it and out.

She drew back in memory to that room always at her fingertips where the details glittered, unmistakable, and said, "Nathan was an archer, and your father made him a small bow and five arrows. The bow was red and the arrows had quail feathers. Deborah loved to sing, so I let her nap outside, under the tree. Zachary was taken from my breast. I'd wrapped him in a blue blanket that morning when your father took him from me. He was our first. The blanket is buried there," she pointed. And Isaac wept with his mother.

Many days Isaac and Sarah walked to the field of flowers and many times he asked her about his brothers and sister, to hear again the details, which she gave to him unaltered, day after day, the exactness of the repetition holding him like a protecting veil.

He learned from her that love sees the other and pays attention to what it sees and he wanted to be like Sarah. Of the flowers that grew by the fence, he asked, "What are these?"

"Carnations," she answered. "See how their petals are variegated, being both red and white?" And he did see.

"And these?"

"Butterflies," she said.

"TELL ME ABOUT myself," Isaac finally asked because he could not see himself clearly either. Much of the time he didn't feel visible at all.

He studied her carefully as she spoke, memorizing her words because they felt like news to him and they were news.

"Well," she began, "your knees are a bit bony but your arms are very strong." He looked down at his body. "You cry out in your sleep and you have every night since you came down from the mountain." He returned to her eyes, binding himself to them. "When you were young, you liked spiders and frogs," she smiled.

They waited a long time. Then he asked, "Am I here?"

"Of course you are here, Isaac. You're right here with me." She reached out both hands and touched the sides of his face. "These are your two ears," she said. "And these, your two eyes." She laid her hands on his lashes, then continued to his ankles and feet. "You are Isaac, my son. My beloved."

Many days they went to the field and Isaac asked her to do the same thing, never tiring of being seen and being touched by her at the same time. "You have two ears, two eyes. You are here, Isaac," she said. "Feel the sun on the backs of your hands? Feel it warming the top of your head?" And he tried to learn it.

WHEN SHE DIED, he grieved for her in the field where he lay in great stillness, studying the red and the white of the carnations, the rough wood of the fence, the flight of the butterflies and told himself, "I am Isaac. I am here. And I am real."

ONE DAY AS he slept, he saw a fountain glistening in the sun, and on it, three youths. Their heads were bent down, their arms crossed over their chests and he recognized them as his brothers and sister even though they all looked exactly the same. He remembered when he lay strapped firm to the stones that his father looked down but didn't really see him there. His eyes were glazed and intent, as if seeing something with a painful clarity that Isaac was not part of, something more real than Isaac and the stones and the wood, the fire and the blade.

ISAAC MEDITATED ON the fountain and wondered if this was how his father saw each of his brothers and his sister when they, too, were on the mountain. That they lay under a film through which their father saw only the innocence he desperately wanted. And Isaac wondered if in those moments, knife in the air, they each had disappeared from his view as he had disappeared. That they were each only a passageway for their father. And he considered, then, that sometimes violence is not even personal, which was another wounding. And he saw, given its power to blind, that the hunger for innocence in an adult can be the most dangerous hunger.

9

Isaac and Rebekah

S EEING THE SEVERE immobility of his son, that he stayed days and nights alone in the field, Abraham sent his servant to find a good wife for Isaac.

REBEKAH LOVED ISAAC and when he took her out to the field and said, "Lie on me, cover me," she did. When he said, "Tell me who I am," she said, "You are Isaac, son of Abraham and Sarah, and husband to me, Rebekah." She learned to touch him, saying, "Here are your eyes, Isaac. Here are your ears." And in this way, she drew him to her so that, in time, Isaac came to love Rebekah.

He loved her even later when they had two sons and she deceived him over the birthright, which she did without pity. Isaac thought, greed isn't everything. And it isn't the worst thing. So he found that it was easy to forgive her. Partly because even in deceiving him, she was strong and purposeful, and so was like his mother had been on the day she dressed her hair with belts of velvet and

wore her fur-trimmed coat and, standing firm, spoke the words
that stopped his father.

10

Moses and the Burning Bush

H E WATCHED THE bush burn without being consumed and was mesmerized because he saw motion and stillness held together as one thing. He rushed toward it despite his age and sore legs, then heard a voice and, fearful, stopped and took off his shoes.

WHEN, FINALLY, HE climbed down from the mountain, people pointed, pulled back, cheered, exclaimed that his face shone like the sun. Light radiated from his body with each step, the dull sand sparkled under his feet. Light came from his fingers, his toes. He told himself, at last, I am aflame with love! At night, in his bed, under the sheets, he checked. It was true. His body glowed. "I bore you up on eagles' wings and brought you to myself," he heard God say.

Panting, he returned the next day and then a third, but saw only roots and sand. He took off his sandals but heard no voice. Through each hour of daylight then evening then night then the moon, he waited and in the morning walked home. A week passed. It was always the same. Two weeks then three. No voice, no flame. Nothing.

EVENTUALLY, HE STOPPED climbing the mountain. His face felt cool again.

Looking in the mirror, he saw only his thinning hair, his slack shoulders, the glow gone. His family and friends jeered, resented his privilege, bitter that it hadn't produced anything new for them. Had produced nothing useful at all.

He knew if he let disappointment come, he would crumble, so he told himself, it's better this way. Perhaps the invisibility of God is a sign of mercy. Not only mercy but *magnam misericordiam*. Great mercy. He tapped the smooth surface of the glass, as if for persuasion, and said, "The Almighty was perfect when he was invisible. Actually, I am relieved. The Almighty was so . . ." he searched for the word, "so *particular*."

DAILY, HE DEMONSTRATED to himself that fire does, in fact, consume what it burns. He liked to strike the match, to set the wood aflame. He sat outside doing nothing else. Liked to watch until the twigs burned to ash.

Over time he set many things on fire, pieces of furniture, wooden cups. He moved his bed outside, kept a fire burning day and night, constantly feeding it. This straw, this torn blanket, this chair, this picture frame.

THEY LET HIM drift, alone, apart. His clothes smelled of smoke. He smeared ashes on his face, filled his mouth with ashes, coated his tongue, his ears, rubbed ashes on his eyelids, hoping to rub away the memory of what was too sweet to carry. And in this way delivered himself back to the world as he had known it. He told himself, there is no mountain, there is no God.

He felt the certainty of the world he had created, certain in all of its smallness. A flat, diminished world but one that comforted him, no longer forced to see all of the ways he was not like the God. No longer forced to see all the ways he failed at love.

But at the same time a voice inside called out,

> *Miserere mei, Deus, secundum magnam misericordiam tuam.*

> Pity me, O God, according to Thy great mercy.

11

Manna

M OSES LED HIS people out of bondage in Egypt where they
had lived for five hundred years. He led them out together,
six hundred thousand on foot. But in time they murmured, saying,
"When God struck the rock, water swept down in torrents. But
can he also give us bread?"

This angered God but an angel came, saying, "Give them bread
from Heaven. Remember, you are the spring of holiness."

So God put on a chiton the color of hoarfrost and when he came
down from Heaven his chiton covered the land. He rained food on
them like dust, in their midst and all around their tents so that, day
after day, they could eat the bread of angels. And God was happy
and no longer vexed with his people because he gave them all that
they craved and told himself, "They will remember my kindness
and will know that they are my people and I am their God."

BUT IN TIME they lamented again, saying, "We remember the
fish we used to eat without cost in Egypt, and the cucumbers, the

melons and leeks, the onions and garlic. Now we have nothing to look forward to but this manna. If only we had meat!"

And God's anger kindled again toward his people. But he overcame his anger and called the quail and they came to him. And he said, "They will eat bread in the morning and flesh in the evening and in that way they will know that I am the Lord their God."

For forty years there was no lack and each person had his fill.

BUT GOD'S ANGER was not hidden from his people and when they told the story of the manna and the quail, and when they wrote it down in sacred books, his anger came more and more to the fore. In the first version, they said, "He gave meat until it came out of the nostrils and was loathsome to his people." And in the next version, that a plague caused death to those who gathered too much manna or quail. In the beautiful book of Psalms, the last version, they wrote, ". . . before they had sated their craving, while the food was still in their mouths, God's anger rose and he slew the strongest among them. He struck down the flower of Israel."

God saw that his anger was there when the story of the manna was written on stone tablets. It was there when the plants that grew in the Nile were picked and the fibers soaked and dried under weight, his violence preserved on the long papyrus rolls. He saw it later when papyrus sheets were folded into quires and the quires made into codices. His anger there when papyrus gave way to vellum and then to parchment. And he despaired, thinking, is this how memory works in my people? That my anger is neither forgiven nor forgotten but is held like a treasure that grows in them over time?

He lifted the hem of his chiton to caress the quail embroidered there, admiring their black plumes, their plump bodies and dainty beaks, then he let them go so that they flew off the garment and walked on the ground around his feet. "Did I send scorpions to my people?" he asked them. "No, I sent you, my sweet ones." But he wondered, why do they think my anger prevails above all else?

He took off his chiton and his himation of indigo blue and sat naked on the bench wondering, are they right? Is this who I am? Am I a God without mercy?

12

Moses and Memory

G OD SAID TO Moses, "My people love me then they don't. They come to me then they forsake me. I want to bind them to myself. I want to make my presence permanent among them."

Moses, hearing fear in the voice of God, asked, "What would you have me do?"

"Listen to me and tell my people everything you hear. For you, Moses, are the Great Rememberer."

God began, his voice robust and determined, and Moses sat back to memorize each word as it came from his mouth. "I am the Lord thy God, who brought you out of the land of Egypt, out of the house of bondage. . . . Thou shalt have no other gods before me. . . . Thou shalt not make unto thee any graven image. . . . Thou shalt not take the name of the Lord thy God in vain. . . ."

And Moses went down the mountain and told the people the words God had spoken and they said in one voice, "This we will do."

THEN GOD CALLED Moses to the mountain a second time and the energy of God was greater than the first and he spoke faster, saying, "If you buy an Hebrew servant, six years he shall serve, and in the seventh year he shall go out free for nothing." And then, "If the servant came in by himself, he shall go out by himself; if he were married, then his wife shall go out with him."

The commands were more detailed, causing Moses to work harder remembering them. "And if the servant shall plainly say, 'I love my master, my wife, and my children, I will not go out free,' then his master shall bring him unto the judges. . . . And if a man sell his daughter to be a maidservant, she shall not go out as the menservants do. If she please not her master, who hath betrothed her to himself, then shall he let her be redeemed. . . ."

God spoke still faster, "And if he have betrothed her unto his son, he shall deal with her after the manner of daughters. . . ." But the cadence, the rhythmic repetition and steady hopefulness in God's voice took Moses away from him and his mountain and into the cave of memory, black and damp and gently rocking, where he slept. Then suddenly a blast of light, something long poking him, bright orange, the basket rocking wildly, a white feathered head, two black eyes then gone.

"If he take him another wife," Moses came back, "her food, her raiment, and her duty of marriage shall he not diminish. And if he do not these three unto her, then shall she go out free without money."

Under the words Moses heard, "Remember this. Remember me, Moses," and he had compassion for God and tried harder, with all of his strength, to remember each word, harnessing himself to them.

"And if a man smite the eye of his servant . . . if an ox gore a man or a woman . . . if a man shall open a pit and not cover it . . . if a man shall cause a field or vineyard to be eaten by his beast . . . if a fire break out and catch in thorns so that the stacks of corn be consumed . . . if a man deliver unto his neighbor an ass and it die . . . if a man entice a maid that is not betrothed . . ."

But Moses dozed off again, hearing only, ". . . and . . . and . . . and . . . and . . ."

The egret, the enormous beak, the rocking of his back against the blanket, the inside of the basket, that it smelled of reeds.

INSIDE THE MEMORY of the basket and the egret, another memory lay, and Moses turned away from God's voice to find it. Further back. At the beginning.

Breath came down on the crown of his head. Skin against skin. A steady rise and fall of his body held from behind and below. His mother's skin, that it smelled of moss.

And Moses could see why God wanted to be bound to his people forever, as he was bound, in memory, to her.

13

Moses and the Dream
of the Law

MOSES STAYED ON the holy mountain because he saw that God needed him. For forty days he listened to the voice of God and learned that God was boundless and not like man, never tiring, inexhaustible.

"If men strive and so hurt a woman with child so that her fruit depart from her, and yet no mischief follow, he shall be surely punished. . . . And if any mischief follow, then thou shalt give life for life, eye for eye, tooth for tooth, hand for hand."

And Moses pitied the desperateness of God, frantic with desire.

". . . gold and silver and brass and blue and purple and scarlet and fine linen and goats' hair and rams' skins dyed red, and badgers' skins and shittim wood, oil for the light spices for anointing oil and for sweet incense, onyx stones and stones to be set in the ephod, and in the breastplate. And let them make me a sanctuary, that I may dwell among them . . . ten curtains of fine twined linen

. . . curtains of goats' hair, the length of the curtain shall be thirty cubits . . . covering of rams' skins dyed red and badgers' skins . . . a veil of blue and purple and scarlet . . . pillars round the court shall be filleted with silver, their hooks of silver, sockets of brass . . ."

Moses began to dream again of sleep. The lep-lep sound of the water when the egret walked away, the sound of the water when it lifted its feet. But he heard, "Remember me. Remember me, Moses," even in his sleep and grew frightened then that he would be on the mountain forever. That God's desire was infinite and his speaking would never end.

"And thou shall make a candlestick of pure gold . . . six branches shall come out of the sides of it, three branches out of the candlestick out of the one side, three branches of the candlestick out of the other side. . . ."

Until finally he screamed, "No more!"

And God stopped.

HE HEARD GOD catch his breath then slow himself until he finally saw the trees bending gently, the grass also bending to the left then to the right then to the left again in the breath of God.

And Moses said, "Show me your glory. I need to see you. I need to see your face."

But God said, "If you see my face, you will die."

"Show me anyway," Moses answered.

GOD WAITED. THEN said, "I will make all my glory pass before you. But I will cover you with my hand and then will take my hand away and you will see the back of my body but not my face, and in that way you will live."

So God covered the eyes of Moses with his hand and passed by Moses in all of his glory. And when he had passed by, he lifted his hand and Moses opened his eyes and saw the back of God. He saw the back of God walking away, the deep blue velvet of his robe spangled with stars like gold dust, uncountable. And Moses saw that the mind of God was orderly and that in his wishes for the candlestick, the incense, the robes of finely woven linen, in his rules for divorce and ownership and property and times and seasons, he was trying to bring his people to holiness. And Moses no longer feared God.

In the morning he would go down from the mountain and write every word that God had said. And he would call God's rulings and instructions, "The Law."

BUT FOR NOW, he stared at the back of God and realized that what had seemed like the infinite neediness of God was its opposite. All night long he stared at the sky and saw that each star was an opening. And he heard God saying, "Come to me. I have given you infinite doors. Pick one and come to me. Enter into the fullness of my mercy."

14

The Queen of Sheba

THE QUEEN OF Sheba, seeking to understand the difference between prayer and magic, healing and sorcery, wisdom and superstition, found her counselors wanting and hearing of the fame of Solomon concerning his god, made a journey of one thousand miles to pose her questions to him.

She traveled with a great train of camels bearing spices, gold, and precious stones. And when she saw his forty thousand stalls of horses and twelve thousand horsemen, the meat at his table, the sitting of his servants, the attendance of his ministers and their apparel, his cupbearers and the way he ascended into the house of his god, she grew faint and offered Solomon all that she had brought, nine thousand pounds of gold and more spices than anyone had ever given the king.

When he drew her away privately, she told him all the questions in her heart. "I've hid nothing from you now," she confessed, and Solomon said, "You are a seeker."

"Give me food to eat," she answered, and he gave her the laws of Moses.

For many days she stayed in the household of the king where she remained in her room reading and did not come out. She saw the Law as a form of love, that each situation was anticipated and provided for, a kind of Mother.

WHEN AT LAST she reappeared Solomon sang to her, accompanied by the harp, speaking as if he were Wisdom herself, saying, "I was there when God prepared the heavens. . . . I was by him and was daily his delight. . . ."

And the Queen asked, "Can this god be known?"

ON THE DAY of her leaving, Solomon gave her eight packets each tied with a gold thread, a song he'd written, and asked her not to read them until she reached home. I will grow in wisdom and be like Solomon, she thought. I will rule with Wisdom and I will come to know his god.

In the cool of her palanquin, she slept with the chaplets under her pillow. The days were long, the nights longer, the trip seemed without end. Borne on the shoulders of a dozen men, she wished instead to be on her own horse, racing home. In the last hundred miles she ordered that they travel at night also, men carrying torches on either side, rotating the porters. The camels, freed of their burden, ran ahead. Still, her bed, the couch and curtain, nothing seemed to move fast enough.

BEFORE EXITING THE palanquin she opened the first packet. He'd written in the voice of a woman saying, "The king hath brought me into his chambers . . . my spikenard sends forth the smell thereof. A bundle of myrrh is my well-beloved unto me; he shall lie all night between my breast." Quickly she hid the chaplet under her skirt.

She untied the second. "He brought me to the banqueting house, and his banner over me was love." In her garden, apple trees espaliered against the thick warm walls, she read, "His left hand is under my head, and his right hand doth embrace me." She dreamt of Solomon's god but also of him.

In haste she opened the third packet and read, "Behold Solomon's bed. Threescore valiant men are around it, the valiant of Israel. . . . Behold king Solomon with his crown." And she pictured his bedroom and wanted to be there with him.

By the fourth chaplet, she realized he'd written her a love letter. There seemed to be no other way to receive his words. "Your two breasts are like two young roes that are twins, which feed among the lilies. Until the daybreak . . . I will get me to the mountain of myrrh, and to the hill of frankincense." She stopped for breath and looked out the window at the two swans in the lake she had built. The pair seemed so happy now. "Honey and milk are under your tongue and the smell of your garments is like the smell of Lebanon." She smelled her perfumed linen, the sachets she had rotated daily in her closets. "Blow upon my garden," he had her ask. "Let my beloved come into his garden and eat his pleasant fruit."

Neglecting her duties, her ministers, visitors, she neglected everything but the horizon, the lake, and the swans. I will graft myself onto you, dear Solomon, my kingdom to yours, all that I have.

Quickly she opened the fifth. "I am my beloved's and my beloved is mine. . . . Return, return." She called her maidservant. They laid out traveling clothes.

The seventh book she read in private, behind the drape. "I will go up to the palm tree, I will take hold of its boughs . . . . Make haste, my beloved, and be thou like a roe or a young hart on the mountains of spices."

She should send word. But, no, she would just go.

"Rise up, my love, my fair one, and come away. . . ." She would take no gifts. "The time of the singing of birds is come, and the voice of the turtle is heard in our land. The fig tree putteth forth her green figs. . . ." Just her maidservant, her cook, manservants and guardsmen. "Arise, my love, my fair one, and come away." She rode her choice Arabians at top speed, a fresh horse every thirty miles, day and night, the mounted torchmen, across the desert in the moonlight.

They would marry, she would wear a diadem studded with topaz and bear many sons and daughters. She already saw them on the ridges of the hills where the goats played. Noble, they would be a beautiful race because they would shape their lives on the Law, all of life flourishing, covenants honored, the widow, the orphan. God would bless them as he was blessing Solomon, festooned in all his glory.

THE MINISTERS WHO went ahead to announce her approach returned ashen. They begged her to turn back but she refused and hastened without even bathing to the court of the king.

But Solomon did not greet her.

She returned the second day. And then the third. At last her ministers found courage to relay the news. Solomon had seven hundred wives and three hundred concubines. They were his when she had first visited, when she'd stayed in his household, when they'd spoken candidly. They were there when he'd given her the song he'd composed at their parting. Moabite women, Ammonites, Edomites, Hittites and Zidonians. He worshipped their gods, Ashtoreth and Milcom, had built temples in their honor where he burned incense and made sacrifices. When pressed, they reported he had "threescore queens and virgins without number."

STRICKEN, SHE RETURNED to Sheba and sequestered herself where she mourned the king and the God of Moses he'd abandoned. Mourned for herself and for what she might have become.

SHE THOUGHT OFTEN of Solomon, that surely at some earlier time there was a condition in which he'd been held but from which, somehow, he had fallen. She wanted to name that prior condition. The name must be beautiful like the embrace of the lovers he'd so well described, like the two swans on her lake, their purity as they glided on the water and sometimes their long necks intertwined, like Wisdom. And she called the condition in which she thought he was held when she first met him and stayed in his rooms, but from which he had fallen, taking with him only appearance, "Grace."

SOMETIMES SHE HEARD the reeds say, "There is a new Bridegroom," and sometimes, "The God of Moses is yours." But she discerned over time that it wasn't the swans speaking and it wasn't the reeds. It was Reason.

"The dry bough bears flower," Reason said.

"But I have no one," she answered.

"Prepare yourself so you may see the immortal Bridegroom and the Kingdom of Heaven be yours."

"But I'm not one of them."

Then Reason said, "Grace is for all, even the foreigner."

And the queen believed these words.

THE NEXT MORNING she powdered her face with lavender and came from her confinement wearing a diadem of laurel leaves, singing,

> *Sanctus, Sanctus, Sanctus*
> *Lord God of hosts.*

SHE PROCLAIMED A Jubilee so that slaves regained their freedom. She had a psalter made.

> *Let every thing that has breath*
> *praise the Lord.*

She appointed judges and gathered her people and read them
the words of Moses once every year, saying,

> *Ecce mater nostra Jerusalem . . .*
> *See how your mother, Jerusalem,*
> *cries with deep emotion, saying:*
> *Come, come to me!*

15

Jonah

G OD SPOKE TO Jonah, the son of Amittai, saying, "Arise,
go to Nineveh, that great city, and cry against it, for their
wickedness has come up before me." But Jonah did not rise up
and instead lay in his bed dreading another city. He knew what
God wanted him to say. Tell them their city will be overthrown in
forty days. He had done it before many times. Over and over God
had sent him to cities, starting with the small ones, villages at first,
then larger. And over and over Jonah did as God had asked. He'd
frightened them then waited to see if they would repent.

It was different in the beginning when God let him preach
repentance, too, and that he didn't mind. He could say, "Your
city will be destroyed unless you repent." And some of them did
repent, and Jonah felt good about his job then, saving the inhabitants and bringing about a reconciliation with God and the people.
It was gratifying and they loved Jonah for warning them, and
esteemed him as a prophet. He had built his reputation that way,
almost a savior.

But lately God was asking him to preach destruction only so that Jonah felt used by God, that he was part of God's testing people to see if, on their own, they would think of repenting. So that he dreaded God's voice and dreaded going to work, dreaded packing his bags and saying good-bye. His wife didn't know what to say to console him because he was a good man, a holy man, but, increasingly, an angry man, too.

Either the inhabitants of the city would realize repentance was necessary, and be saved, or they would not, and it was painful for Jonah to see all the deaths of those who did not think to repent. God testing greater and greater populations, so that now God had set his heart on Nineveh, to test that metropolis, the greatest city Jonah had ever seen.

It also seemed to him that God loved repenting of his anger. First feeling it then changing his mind and repenting of it. He seemed dependent on it and this need in God had troubled Jonah for some time. Jonah came to feel separate from his own conscience, allowed to say, "Your end is coming!" but not to make clear the only remedy. It seemed a trick, finally, to Jonah and he felt defiled by it. As if he was being dragged around by God and his ever-increasing need to be loved.

Jonah had also grown hardened by all the deaths he had witnessed. It sat heavy on him at first, but then he grew indifferent, immoveable, his heart so cold that he could see suffering and feel nothing, see his own child fall and feel nothing, see his wife mourning the death of her mother and feel nothing, the widower next door who often had no bread, no oil for his lamp, and feel nothing.

It was Jonah's safety and this frightened his wife who missed the man she had married. They had vowed to love each other until death, and Jonah seemed dead to her already and he felt dead.

WHEN GOD ASKED him to go to Nineveh, Jonah fled in the opposite direction, defying God, but feeling wonderful as he ran. He boarded a ship to Tarshish and paid the fare and went down into its hold and slept better than he had in many years.

But God caused a great wind to whip the sea, a tempest so great that the ship would be broken by it and the mariners were afraid and while Jonah slept peacefully each cried out to his own god for deliverance. Seeing no result and desperate, they frantically cast their wares into the sea to lighten the ship's load. But the wind did not diminish and then they feared for their lives.

Indignant and furious, the captain of the ship came down to Jonah and asked, "What are you doing?" He commanded Jonah to call out to his god like they each had so that the crew and the ship would not perish. "What is your name?" he asked. "And your occupation? Where are you from and why are you here with us?"

Jonah saw terror on the face of the captain but felt nothing. He learned that the sailors had cast all their wares into the sea and felt nothing for them either. Calmly he told the captain that he was a Hebrew, that his god had made the heaven and the earth, the sea and the dry land, and with candor said he was fleeing the presence of his god at that very moment. Finding his life a trifle, Jonah said, "Cast me into the sea. The wind will die down then, immediately." Without remorse, he added, "I am the cause of all of this." And he prepared for his death, looking forward to it, to the integrity of that final act.

But the captain and crew didn't want to cause the death of a man who seemed otherwise innocent, so they rowed hard to bring the ship to land and could not. Only then did they beseech their gods to not hold Jonah's innocent blood against them, and took Jonah up and cast him into the sea. And the sea became still.

Jonah fell to the depths, to the bottoms of the mountains there, seaweed wrapped his hair but he did not die as he had hoped. Instead God had prepared a great fish to swallow Jonah and it did, and Jonah was in the belly of the fish three days and three nights.

I CAN STAY here for the rest of my life and be content, Jonah told himself, in that basilica of bones, the thunderous heartbeat in the thick fleshy red walls, the constant passing of water in and out, up to his shoulders in it, the whale's long, lonely cries that went on hour after hour. Because he had not preached to Nineveh what God had commanded, Jonah felt peace.

But on the third day he woke to the sound of thrashing, the wet floor of muscle, the grid of bone wildly rocking, the upward pull so that he could barely keep his balance, then the bright sun, his arms outstretched, flying through the air, the cold wind, the waves beneath him until he fell to the sand. And Jonah remembered that his power was not the same as God's power. And that he didn't even have power over his own life, and in despair he resigned himself to this.

He knew what God would want to hear, the sweetness God longed for. So he said the words as he lay on the sand, sore and bruised. He said them by rote, without conviction, "I cried because of my affliction to you, Lord, and you heard me. Out of the belly of Hell I cried, and you heard my voice." Then he lied to please God further, saying, "You cast me into the deep," which was not true because Jonah had asked to be thrown overboard. But God did not correct him and this troubled Jonah. He continued, "The floods compassed me about, and I said, 'I am cast out of thy sight.' Yet, I will look again toward your holy temple. When my soul fainted I remembered the Lord and my prayer came in unto thee," which also was not true because he had not prayed to God at all. Then to finish he said, "Salvation belongs to you," which he knew God longed to hear. And God received Jonah's words with joy, which saddened him even more, that God could no longer discern the matters of his heart.

But then Jonah said something that he did believe. He called after God, yelling it as an insult, but also because it was true. Yelling to bring candor back, as it had marked their times together in the early years. "They that observe lying vanities," he screamed, "forsake their own mercy!" But God kept walking away.

JONAH RETURNED HOME to the sullenness of his wife, to the distance of his daughter, to the meaninglessness of his life, and spoke nothing about his journey or his time in the whale or that he finally accused God of his vanity. That mercy paid the price.

THEN THE WORD of God came to Jonah a second time regarding Nineveh. "Arise," Jonah heard in the night. And he felt sickened by the voice that would not leave him alone. He dreaded what he knew would follow, and it did follow. God's vanity not satisfied, Nineveh still tempting him. "Go to Nineveh," God said, again, "that great city." Jonah heard the sighing of God as a kind of lust. "And preach to it the preaching I bid you." Jonah felt the noose tightening.

He looked again at his wife and child, knowing he was powerless against such a god and he packed his bags.

IT WAS AN exceedingly great city and after walking one day toward its center Jonah began to preach. "In forty days Nineveh will be overthrown." He didn't speak loudly or with zeal. He couldn't rouse himself even though thousands would perish. When he finished preaching he went outside the city and there built himself a small booth and sat under it in the shadow, waiting to see what would happen. Either God would destroy the vast and beautiful city of Nineveh, or, by some miracle, they would come to repentance and the city would be spared. If spared he would be called a false prophet, one whose words were not true.

TO HIS SURPRISE, the people of Nineveh proclaimed a fast and put on sackcloth, every man, woman, and child. And when his words reached the king, the king himself rose from his throne, laid aside his robe and covered himself with sackcloth. He sat in ashes and promulgated a decree saying, "Let neither man nor beast, herd nor flock, taste anything. Let them not feed or drink water. But let man and beast be covered with sackcloth and cry mightily unto

God, turning from their evil ways and from the violence in their hands." This astonished Jonah. Beasts in sackcloth and ashes, cows fasting, chickens and pigs. "Who can tell if God will turn away from his fierce anger so that we not perish?" the king ventured.

With those last words Jonah knew that God had the best of what he desired. The rest was predictable. God saw their repentance and repented himself of the evil he had said he would do to them. And he did not destroy the great city of Nineveh.

JONAH RAGED AGAINST God, who was, at that time, so pleased. "Take my life from me!" he implored, but God would have none of it.

"Is it good for you to be so angry?" he asked Jonah almost coyly, and Jonah hated God then, his neediness, his vanity, his predictability and lust.

It was day, the sun hot on Jonah despite his booth, and God caused a gourd to grow up over Jonah to increase the shade, saying, "This will deliver you from your grief," and hearing this Jonah felt even further from the God he once loved.

The gourd and the vine cooled Jonah and Jonah felt for the gourd all the love he'd once felt for his wife and daughter and for God himself, the gourd bringing all this to Jonah so that he loved the gourd deeply and cried because he could again feel such things.

But in the morning he saw that a worm had killed the gourd and that the vine had withered and Jonah sensed that God was behind this, that he had brought the worm. And Jonah broke down and wept bitterly for the helpless gourd. He wept for all the people in cities and villages who had perished because his words weren't enough to direct them to repentance. He cried for his wife and child whom he no longer knew. He cried for the mariners and the possessions they'd thrown overboard on his account, and for the whale who had generously housed him. He cried for all the people every day of his life for whom he felt nothing. And he cried because the repentance of Nineveh was so complete, even the cows and sheep and horses cloaked in sackcloth. He'd never seen such a beautiful show of contrition, the gourd so helpless, the leaves of the vine crushing in his hand.

He wanted to bury it properly but a vehement east wind came and the sun beat on his head so that he fainted and he thought, maybe this time I won't wake.

But God woke him and said, "Is it good that you have pity on the gourd?"

And Jonah gathered all his strength and screamed, "Yes! It is good that I can weep and be angry and that I have pity on the gourd!"

"Well," God sighed, "don't you think I should have spared Nineveh, that great city, with more than six-score inhabitants who can't discern between their right hand and their left, and much cattle?" At this Jonah fell even deeper into despair, which he thought was impossible, disgusted to hear God again refer to the greatness of Nineveh, to the size of its population, even the cattle, because they too had given him what he craved.

JONAH SAT UP then stood and cried out, "I am done with you! I am sick of this! I've become a jester. A harlequin, don't you see? I want an ordinary life. To be like the mariners. I want my wife and daughter. I want to go home!"

And with that God let him go.

CASTING ABOUT, KNOWING he must find a replacement, for his need was great, God wondered where he would find a prophet as powerful as Jonah.

WHEN HE RETURNED to his wife and child, Jonah took off his diamond suit and threw it into the trash. He and his wife began to speak to each other again about important things. When Jonah told her about God's limitless hunger she asked, "What did you say?"

"I am no longer your prophet. I want to go home." And she loved him robustly because he was a man of integrity again. "I couldn't believe in him anymore," Jonah said, taking her hand as they sat on the edge of the bed.

"If you're no longer his prophet," she asked, "what will you be?"

They sat, leg against leg, rubbing each other's fingers, getting re-acquainted. Admitting the term was new for them, and that it had an unusual sound to it, he told her, "I will be God's atheist."

They sat a long time and Jonah felt clean and refreshed. He felt, at last, home.

WHEN THEY STOOD at the door and looked at their daughter who was sleeping in her bed, Jonah saw that the story of his life would be told in a different way than he had lived it, if it was told at all.

It would become the story of a prophet who rebelled against God then repented. There would be nothing of his sense of debasement or the coldness of his heart that the job came to require. Others would not see, as God had not seen, why he wept so bitterly at the death of the gourd. He likely would never be understood by anyone except by his wife, for which he was grateful, and he thought such not-understanding was perhaps the human condition in general. And this pleased him, to be like others, to be part of what was experienced by well-meaning people of all kinds, rather than preaching against them.

As his wife bathed him and washed his hair, he saw a future in which icons would be painted showing him coming out of the mouth of a great fish. He would be painted standing upright with a scroll in his hand and the words on the scroll would be the words he'd said to God halfheartedly, by rote. There was nothing he could do to prevent this. But he wished those who would devoutly paint him would give him truer words, more his own, so that the scroll would read, simply, "I wanted a better God."

II.

1

The Annunciation

PERHAPS IT WAS like this—

THE DRAPE OF her dress on the kneeling board, hands crossed over her breast, in prayer or reading. Maybe asleep. She did not invite him in.

Of course she was terrified. Of course she jumped back and gripped the wall. Threw books at him. Said, "Don't ask such things of me! To carry a child, unwed. To risk death by stoning." And he, the difficult child, the unknown one. "No! Get out!"

Perhaps he left. Came back. The Angel Annunciate.

"STOP BOTHERING ME!" she might have said. Thinking, if I even listen to you, I will come undone. His light, his voice. As of another world. A world past sand and crow. Past the laundry drying in the tree.

Why did I think it was an easy thing? A moment of terror and then consent. How could it be? Years, years to do that work. To look into an unknown world, past lake and market smell, the fish, their hammered heads, the thud, that sound of her father working, her mother grinding almonds between stone, just so, that flick of the water from her fingertips, that bit of oil. The paste. The angel leaving, coming again.

PERHAPS HE LEARNED to make the sound of knocking, learned to wait until she said, "Come in," before he let go his celestial light. His nimbus brighter than the sun. Perhaps he learned to stay on the far side of the room, hands at his sides. His wing against the wall. They eyed their differences. All that lay between. So that, in time, she came to mark the distance on the floor between where he always stood and where she sat. Forty inches and three quarters. A new, unchanging, sacred space. In time, coming to know the shadow on the floor, cast from his light, to be her own. Many times into her room. Perhaps seventy times seven.

YEARS, YEARS, TRYING to see how she was separate from her friends, the water in the well, the raven, her mother's hand, the dust on the stony ledge. Until she knew her own outline, how could she let another in? "Go! Get out of here!" And he, vacating through the wall. His trace, his feather, on the cold clay floor.

She put it in her basket with the others.

The first ones, when Gabriel was young and confident. Proud of his charge. Proud of his vocation. The cobalt blue, the radiating green of the wing. In those days, when his entrance lit up her room.

Now she barely notices when he is there. His grey wings, travel-worn and weary. The fatigue she sees in his eyes. His clumsiness. A jar knocked over by mistake. His wrinkled, callused feet. His tattered nimbus now a simple crown of fish.

Patient, the patient angel. His weathered wing. His mission not accomplished. His old age, his worry. Shame.

Among the angelic choir, silence when he passes by. The Crazy Angel, they call him, The One Who Doesn't Give Up. Grey winged, blue eyed. The gentle one. He waits long. Returning. Leaving again. His life that is no longer remarkable. Frayed. Dull.

Did she have a violation? A memory? A wound? A cave inside big enough to hold the problem child? What wound could this be? Perhaps only when she remembered it, would there be room.

The day when her work was finished, long, since that first visit when she threw the books, she speaks to him. Knowing to speak louder than before. His diminished hearing, his eyes cloudy, the whites yellowed with age. "I have a ripped-apart place," she tells him. "I am ready. I have enough room."

He raises his tired eyes. He spreads his wings, wide, against the wall. His nimbus fills with light.

"Behold," she instructed him. "See before you the handmaid of the Lord."

2

Annunciation, II

O R, PERHAPS IT was like this—

MARY AT THE well turned her head in the direction of the voice.
Listening, her feet trembled in her black shoes.
Stay still, she told herself. Someone is putting roses in my hair.
Don't move, not even my fingers.

ALWAYS ALONE, IT came when she was most vulnerable.
Until one day when she screamed, "No! You cannot do that
to me!"

3

The Visitation

S HE RAN.

If Joseph did not believe her and refused to marry, the men of Nazareth would bury her up to her neck in the sand and would kill her, slowly, in a hail of stones. They would volunteer to do this, to be the ones.

She ran into the hills, alone. Ran one hundred miles straight into the arms of Elizabeth.

IN THE DAY Mary rested, almost calm, Elizabeth bringing tea, glass cups rattling on a wicker tray. She had marked pages, set it on the night stand, having read the stories herself, trying to find other women who had conceived in old age like she now had, her body heavy and slow, her breasts enlarged and tender like a young woman's.

Likewise, Mary read to find herself in the stories. But all the women who conceived when it had seemed hopeless were old, not like herself, only fifteen. And the husbands were, in every case, also the fathers.

"There is no precedent," she told Elizabeth. "I have no sisters. I am alone."

THE FEARS RETURNED. Her dreams were vivid. She was a dead mare with her dead foal, carted about by a senseless minotaur.

Sometimes she was a girl with a dove, guiding the minotaur in the night.

A MONTH PASSED and there was no blood. When the second month came, and, again, there was no blood, certainty fell on Elizabeth and she knelt down before Mary, holding the chair for balance, and cried out with a loud voice, "Blessed art thou among women and blessed is the fruit of thy womb!" She laid her palm on Mary's torso, touching what was already there, and for a moment Mary thought, maybe it's true and maybe I am safe. "The child in my womb leaps for joy!" Elizabeth exclaimed, short of breath, "because you, Mary, are the mother of my Lord, and you have come to me."

In that profession of Elizabeth, whom she loved, the rocking boat in which Mary found herself began to settle.

"My soul magnifies the Lord," Mary began, testing how it felt, "and my spirit rejoices in God my Savior. . . ." The more she spoke, the more her own words lifted her up from fear. "Behold, all generations will call me blessed because he who is mighty has done great things for me, and holy is his name." She spoke as if almost knowing that the voice she had so often heard was not dangerous but was God's voice.

WHEN THEY TOLD Zachariah what they had come to believe, he withdrew to his room and when he emerged, still struck with muteness, he wrote questions for Mary. "Is this true?"

"Yes," she replied.

He scribbled the words faster. "You have not been with Joseph?"

"I haven't been with any man."

A firm silence fell over the room, sober and dark. They were all thinking the same thing. "If Joseph doesn't believe and marry me, I will be killed," she said.

Zachariah looked down at the bony white knuckles of his hands and wrote, slowly, with great care, "I will protect you."

"Go home now and tell Joseph," Elizabeth said. "Prepare him."

THROUGH THE HILLS Mary walked slowly this time, to cleave to what Elizabeth and Zachariah had given her. That armor.

By the time she reached home, Elizabeth's child had been born, and, as foretold, it was a boy. In obedience they named him John and speech returned to Zachariah.

Things beyond nature were everywhere happening. Courage would now be the new demand. In this she felt united with holy women everywhere. She heard a woman singing from the future,

O most steadfast path.
O mail-coat of hope.
O sword-belt of honesty.

She called bravely to the Angel Gabriel who came in haste. "See before you," she instructed, as one raising her shield, "the handmaid of the Lord."

4

Joseph's Decision

E'D MISSED HER. Gone three months and no word. He
groomed his hair, his fingernails. "She's coming to me," he
told himself, "the Queen of Galilee."

But she was pregnant when she returned from the hill country
and the only thing he knew for certain was that he was not the
father.

It was God's child? She was talking to angels now? Even the
details didn't make sense. She went without saying good-bye,
didn't tell him or her parents but had just run away.

"Look at my hands, my feet," he exclaimed. "I'm a practical
man! What am I to do?"

It felt new to call himself "a practical man," new to call himself
a man at all. His father had been encouraging him to become more
independent, stronger, more reliable, and he had tried to grow into
this for his father's sake. He was engaged, he and Mary would
have many children, he would stop drifting and apply himself to
his trade. He would build a large family table with many leaves and

Mary would learn to cook, making large pots of lentils, soups and stews. He could picture it. Mary would even teach him to read and teach their children to read, one by one. He would make beautiful, useful objects of wood, writing desks, fine cases, and his business would prosper. Knowing well the various trees and their distinct properties, the work of his life would glorify God and bring honor to his family. But he was not prepared for this.

He unfolded the drawing his father had made for him, of a boy his own age, also sixteen, saying, "He's just like you." Joseph held the picture and practiced standing in front of the mirror being that boy, David with Goliath, his hand on his hip, as if he had no fear. He practiced the boy's cocky pose, the slingshot, the soft boots, the sword, and stood a long time until he could really feel the doubts fall at his feet. His father had drawn the slingshot but also a sword, explaining, "Just in case the stone misses its mark." Then added, "Courage is required for every other virtue, Joseph. Remember that."

For many nights he kept to himself and Mary was shaken by it, her life in the balance and the baby's life, too. But she knew it was his habit to make difficult decisions in sleep and silence, waiting for the authoritative voice that was not his own, the familiar voice that had never done him ill. Living on the film of his dreams.

As he stood practicing bravery, Joseph began to feel supported as if by a sturdy platform made of wood. The platform lifted him and Mary over this difficult time and into another, where they were a bit older, he maybe twenty and Mary nineteen. Mary was again like a dream to him, his queen, alive and real. All the confusion fell

away. In fact, everything fell away except that he loved her. And
she desperately needed to be believed.

And he came out of his room and returned to her. Not twenty
and nineteen but sixteen and fifteen. It didn't matter. They held
each other and, girded with gladness, flew out of the familiar into
the great unknown.

5

The Nativity of Jesus

JOSEPH SAT APART, in a corner. Not because the midwives wanted him out of the way, he'd found them past midnight, frantically knocking on doors, and they'd come quickly, but because doubt had returned and he wasn't ready for it. The journey had been difficult, then shepherds came saying angels were singing in the sky. Nothing was simple, nothing within the reach of his understanding.

He'd called the day they married Bright Friday. It was his favorite day of the week, then Bright Saturday, Bright Sunday. He reasoned, she sees behind a membrane and I don't. I see what's in front of me. She sees the transparent structure of the world and I can't see it. Maybe that's why we're perfect for each other. Besides, we love the same God. That will be enough.

But now the room smelled foul even though he'd washed everything down with buckets of clean water. He'd wanted cleanliness. Then privacy. Now he wanted Mary to look stronger than she did, more able to bring other children into the world. He wished her hips were wider, her breasts more full. Birth from a virgin is not possible, and he wondered when the true father would show up. It could be one of the shepherds for all he knew. Maybe they mocked him.

If God gives us love, why not the necessary courage to sustain it? If God gives courage, why isn't it permanent?

HE STARED AT his knees and did not see Mary, who looked away from the baby and across to him. She felt the presence of his doubts and their power. Afraid, she wondered, are we no longer *us?* In a brief moment of sleep, Joseph walked toward her. He was an old man and as he walked white powder fell from his elbows and knees. She woke with a jolt. The baby was crying. Something is disintegrating, she thought. He is leaving us.

6

Mary Loving-kindness

WHEN SHE HELD Jesus on her knee and he reached his arm around her neck, Mary felt flooded with melancholy she could not account for, a profound foreknowledge of sorrow for which she had no empirical evidence. She saw that what she'd given her son by giving him her body was suffering. And she grieved not only for herself, her son and husband, but for all of creation, the cat outside, the cucumbers sliced in the bowl, the great fish in the sea, vulture and crow, for every person, for lovers, for every child born and yet to come. Grieved for the entire world in all its soiled history and crippled future because suffering was an inalienable element of the world's order and because it was incurable.

From that day on, she resolved to pray hourly for all of creation, the reptiles and insects, the flowers and birds, for those she loved and for those she did not love.

IN TIME A startling vision came to her that was unlike anything she'd ever seen with her eyes. Two hands very near each other. Hers and her son's. And she could not reach him.

THE VISION CAME often so she began to pray for those who would hurt her son and for the enemies of truth. Eventually she was able to pray that her son's enemies, sure that he would have them, would also be preserved and be shown mercy.

She prepared herself, and she would also prepare him.

"What is the price of salvation?" she asked Jesus as he grew, until one day he answered, "Death."

And she said, "Yes."

7

Epiphany

S HE WAS AFRAID when she heard the commotion outside, looked through the latch, and waited. Joseph gone, the moon too bright and, opening the door, she saw that there was no moon.

"My husband will be home any minute," she said. The men looked wise and exotic so she added, "He's a dreamer," hoping they would think more highly of him, and then invited them in. They brought fruitcakes, berries, sweet wine in bottles, gold coins, incense, a bracelet for her. The myrrh she refused.

"No, take it to anoint the dead," one said.

"I know what it's for," she snapped, remembering how she'd anointed her mother.

"No," he insisted, pointing to the boy on the floor surrounded by the new toys, a wooden sword, a ball, a kite. He set it on the table anyway. She would remove it the next day, take it to the riverbank, bury it in the mud.

"IT WAS A miracle," she told Joseph. "They came from so far away!"

He lay down. "What did they want? The neighbors said they were wealthy. Like kings." When he looked at her bracelet, she realized they'd brought nothing for him. "I wish I'd been home," he offered.

She wanted him to decipher the meaning of the visit for her. "Is it a warning?" He shook his head. "I don't know. Did they have wives? Families?"

"They didn't say."

"And they knew you?"

"They were looking for him," she pointed to the young boy.

He has my co-ordination, Joseph thought, seeing how skillfully their son held the ball. It was a small idea but that's why he liked it, a resting place in what had become another conversation he did not understand.

To be an accessory was not a new feeling. He'd felt it when they took Jesus to the temple as an infant. Mary walked ahead holding their baby as if he were hers only, and he followed with nothing but the turtledoves.

From the day the wealthy men came, Joseph oscillated between two interpretations of his life which could not both be true at the same time. And there was no third position. Either the God of Abraham and Isaac had somehow joined himself to the body of his son, his loveable son, or his wife had an imagination that was possibly dangerous. Dangerous for a small boy, putting ridiculous ideas in his head. A woman from whom he should protect his son.

He watched as Mary bathed the boy and dressed him for bed, the cloth tiger, the sword, the puppets, the clutter of it a comfort

and in the clutter of objects he tried to find peace. In the smooth-
ness of Mary's arms, her thin waist, she seemed, again, too frail
and good to abandon. Tonight he would not go away to think. He
would stay home, with them.

He and Mary fell asleep in each other's arms. But Joseph woke
shaking. His dream was full of wailing, galloping horses and blood.

8

The Slaying of Infants

TRASH CANS KICKED over, a door slammed, screaming. Then another voice, one she recognized. The woman with twins. Mary lit the candle, opened the door. A third scream from the butcher's house. Soldiers on horseback. Blood in the street. Lamps coming on all down the block. Screams from the house behind. The slap of leather on flesh. Shadows of horses running across the sides of the houses. And then they were gone. Like horses of the apocalypse, Mary thought.

In daylight all was still. Men and women and children, as if frozen, stared at the street. No blood on the lintels. None on the doors. It wasn't the angel of death. They were soldiers with blankets under their saddles and shields. No one spoke. No one ate. No one moved into action. For days blood lay unanswered in the street.

In almost every house, a dead child and a living one. And all the dead children were boys. All of them young. Older brothers and sisters sleepwalking, dazed, one boy laughed uncontrollably, holding his pet mouse, stroking it.

A WEEK LATER she woke in a pool of blood. It was true, then, she had been with child. Glistening and motionless, she held it in the palm of her hand. It would have been a brother.

It was weeks, when a skin of normalcy returned, that the smart girl did the calculations. Only boys were murdered and only those two years old or younger. The age Jesus had been. By rumor and calculation, pieces were assembled. The order had come down from Herod himself.

"IT WASN'T OUR fault," Joseph repeated.

"But our son was saved and none of the others his age. We were lucky. You had that dream."

Joseph tried to be patient but she'd spoken this way for months, demanding that he console her, demanding that he say again, "It had nothing to do with us." But it didn't help. She would say, "It's because of us," whenever the temperature dropped and the air felt like that night's air. Or the jasmine smelled outside the window as it had that night. Or the stars aligned in the same way.

The families who lost one son and those who lost two threw rocks at their door. At the well, women locked arms forming a barricade so that she fetched water at noon in the sweltering sun when no one was there.

Their outrage did not fade. "We saw our sons murdered and you miscarried!" the women taunted her. "We've all miscarried plenty!" In this the older women chimed in, even the grandmothers, drawing on memory.

Some days Mary wanted neither marriage nor motherhood. Thought, if this is holiness, I don't want any part of it. Unable to feel compassion, unable to forgive, she called out to Joseph, "I don't want to be here anymore!" and Joseph thought, I have nothing left to give you.

"WHY DIDN'T YOU warn us?" the men boycotted his workshop, no customers came so there was, suddenly, no income, just what was left of the gold.

Shunned in public, forbidden to attend the funerals of the slain, Joseph took his goods to other villages where he was not known, but his business did not grow. He found work making small repairs, a stuck drawer, a weakened table leg, a broken gate.

FROM THE CABINET behind the stove she took some of the gold and traveled to Jerusalem where she bought a costly garment. She put it on and stood in front of the mirror. It changed nothing. She wanted to feel innocent and could not.

There would be no more pregnancies. She and Joseph felt unable to be sexual, unable to risk more unhappiness, unable to find in the body of the other either pleasure or solace. The table he built lay almost empty and more children would not come. Over the years he would take the leaves and chop them to kindling.

9

The Murder of Zachariah

ORD CAME FROM the hill country. On the same night that Jesus was spared, soldiers had gone to the house of Elizabeth and Zachariah seeking their child, to slay him. But Zachariah had hidden his wife and son in the wilderness, in a mountain that opened its bosom to them. And when the soldier asked the whereabouts of the child, Zachariah refused to divulge their hiding place and for this was slain along with the infants.

10

Holy Family

F IVE YEARS PASSED and Jesus was seven. Mary set the table and Joseph planned games. She'd made a cake fashioning animals of almond paste for the top, sheep, camels, rabbits, one for each guest, eighteen in all. She felt that they were help mates again, she and Joseph doing the party together. But no children came. Not the older boys, not any of the girls, except, finally, one, the Gentile girl who came with her cat, but seeing the large cake and none of her friends, set down her present and left.

The plates around the table, the favors and party hats, Joseph, Mary, and Jesus held hands. Looking at his wife to make a point, that she not forget it, Joseph said, "We are a *holy* family." She lit the candles and, seeing her husband through them, that he was a person of discernment, a provider of sound judgment, she wondered, is it true? Are we a holy family after all?

As she cut the cake she could almost feel again that surprise when the angel addressed her as an innocent. How at one point he'd looked right into her eyes and she'd looked right into his and consented to what she did not understand because everything he was saying felt both real and good.

JOSEPH SAID THOSE words but did not believe them. I, too, have eaten ashes like bread. He thought of his father's favorite psalm, 137, "They who carried us away required myth of us," and he tried to do this. Then, "If I make my bed in Hell, thou art there." He'd memorized all one hundred and fifty psalms by the time he was his son's age, his father punctuating speech with a psalm day and night, phrases for every mood, happy, dejected, fatigued, energetic.

But he was stretching, to be a holding net, to keep the family together in a claim of innocence that none of them felt. Not Mary, not himself, not their son who'd grown up with the anniversaries, the torchlight processions, the weeping, portraits drawn on the walls in chalk. Families had moved away, many decided they would bring no more children into the world, others divorced, siblings developed strange illnesses. Most no longer observed the Sabbath. "We've sacrificed enough," the boy read on their faces scarred with grief.

Joseph looked at his son and wife and hid his thoughts because, again, he was calculating. The logic came to him often. If he hadn't been a dreamer, if he hadn't obeyed the voice in his dreams, if he hadn't married Mary, she would have been dead seven years now, a thought he despised, as well as their son. But all the other boys would still be alive. Hundreds of them. And Zachariah, too. He said, "We are a holy family," because he said it to himself often, when the calculating came like a fiendish animal circling the bed-post, the front door, his work bench, and he was ashamed.

When he prayed, which was rare, it was to tell God, in case he'd forgotten, "Send me no more of your dreams."

11

Finding Jesus in the Temple

J ESUS SAT BY himself often, trying to understand his family, the murder of his uncle, Zachariah, and the murder of his male peers. He was five, he was eight, he was eleven. He had no answer. Sometimes he wished he'd been murdered, too. At those times he was angry with his father for having dreams and for obeying them. Angry that his father's dreams had twice saved his life.

WHEN HE SPOKE in the Temple, though he was only twelve, he spoke of unhappiness, destiny and the web into which, though we don't design it, we are born. He spoke with great conviction and little emotion. That he knew about human suffering was clear to those who heard him.

HE DIDN'T SPEAK of the night visitors who came bringing gifts. That he still had the kite, his mother, the gold. He spoke of what he'd seen, of the limit of riches to bring happiness, that gold did not lift his mother's despondency when he watched her stand before the mirror newly clothed in fine garments and wept. The dress that still hung at the back of her closet, unworn. Riches could not prevent the slicing off anymore than righteousness could. Her righteousness, his father's, his uncle's, the parents in his neighborhood.

"The Son of Man will bring division," he said because this was the nature of the puzzle he was trying to solve, the severing he'd already seen and had set in motion. A family of four children had three. A family with two sons had only one. That knife blade. That sickle.

"Who is my mother and brother?" Mary quizzed him.

"Those who hear the word of God and do it," he answered and spoke the same that day in the Temple.

Those present listened with amazement and some said, "Surely this boy is a prophet."

AFTER SEARCHING FOR Jesus three days, Joseph and Mary found him in the Temple and Joseph instructed him to come home, but Jesus answered, saying, "*Here* I am doing my father's business," rebuking his father, which offended Joseph. And the Elders, witnessing the exchange, said among themselves, "Is he the boy's father? This carpenter? The one who can't read? The one who makes chairs?"

Mary did not hear the insult, so that Joseph bore the full weight of the humiliation without her.

In that moment he saw the degree of his uselessness to both her and their son and felt anger again toward Jesus. He thought of Abraham's rage against Isaac, a story he knew from childhood, his father telling it to him with sadness, saying, "I hope we never have that strife between us."

His wife and son had eyes fixed on something greater that he could not see, something more important than being a family, even a holy one. And Joseph fell away from them, so that there was no repairing it. Once they reached home, he would gather his possessions and move away.

They seemed unconcerned with happiness, which he held as life's greatest gain, a true measure of the spiritual life. Life was made for joy, after all. And he did not take it for granted much less devalue it as they seemed to do. He looked at them as they walked ahead, feeling how keenly he wanted a simple life, a life without the supernatural in it.

They walked so closely that their steps almost matched, the boy almost as tall as his mother, each occasionally looking away at the landscape, the hills to the left, the wide, flat expanse of sand to the right. By the time they reached home, Joseph wondered if their quest for some higher meaning that he did not feel or feel drawn to was a kind of gluttony or greed.

12

Elizabeth

WOMEN FOUND ELIZABETH noble in her widowhood. Some envied her because her son lived, others because her husband had hidden them, still others because he had given his life for them.

Zachariah achieved remarkable stature among them, his face drawn in chalk on the walls, leading the slain children to a safe place, a beyond. It was a myth in the village, and a comfort, and for Zachariah, each anniversary, the tallest white candles were lit.

The story was singular among the families of the slain and told everywhere on the anniversary of that night, so that at times Jesus envied his cousin.

When Elizabeth dreamt of her husband, which was often, he wore ochre, vermilion and gold, rich fabrics befitting a martyr. She existed as if in his presence so that she saw herself in that same way, on her fingers sapphire and ruby rings where there were none, wearing a crinoline head piece and dressed in an ermine-trimmed gown embroidered in gold.

She existed in this state of mind. Resolute. Unafraid. Composed.

WHEN HE WAS young, she knit John a raven of black yarn and left notes and snacks outside his door, a fig cookie, a paper airplane, "To Elijah from the Raven." It was their game. John knew and loved the story of the prophet fed by ravens in the wilderness and made her tell it again and again. Often he stood on the kitchen chair, pretending to ride up to Heaven in a chariot of fire. He demanded she admire him. "You, my little Thunder-Bearer!" she said playfully.

He cut out large paper wings and she tied them to his arms, first pricking the paper with her needle then pushing through the string. "Oh, you have the wings of a messenger!" she exclaimed as he opened them wide and jumped from the table, calling out, "I'm the Angel of the Wilderness!" then running around the room.

But sometimes she saw streaks of gold on his paper wings and through the window gold on the trees. She watched his feet grow into the shape of the prophet's. She'd seen the paintings. It seemed more than a coincidence. And then, the same elongated, spade-shaped face, so extreme on some days that for a moment it looked like the face of a dog.

She thought, these are ascetic features belonging to one with an austere message, a preacher of penitence.

13

John and Jesus as Children

B OTH FATHERLESS, JESUS and John spent time together, their mothers devoted to each other and to them. Mary made puppets from small pieces of wood, string, scraps of cloth, and they played "Three Kings," riding the rake and broom like camels.

They played games they would not play with other children. "Turn the other cheek," John said, thinking of his father succumbing to the soldier, and Jesus said the same, thinking of the women who barricaded his mother from the well. "When someone strikes you, turn the other cheek," was their code and they played different versions of it, Father and the Soldier, Mother and the Women at the Well. They practiced fighting with swords, one turning the cheek while being slain. Other times they fought to win, loud and shrieking, pretending to stab each other, to fall dead, to be the victor. And sometimes real anger emerged. John crying out, "If it weren't for you, I'd still have my father!"

JESUS ALSO WANTED Zachariah. He imagined growing up to be like him, to give his life for something. A priest in the Temple, then a martyr. To be heroic. To return to the world something that already seemed like a debt.

"People don't become martyrs because they want to be heroic," his aunt instructed him. "They become martyrs because they love something or someone to a heroic degree."

BY THE TIME Jesus was eighteen, his father had been gone six years without coming home. John knew this, yet he envied Jesus because his father lived in some particular place and spoke real words and ate and drank like other men.

Hearing the longing of her nephew, Mary opened the box in which she'd kept the notes Zachariah wrote to her when he could not speak and gave them to John who loved the small papers because they had touched his father.

AS THEY GREW John longed to meet Joseph and begged Jesus to look for him. "Let's find him," he said, wanting touch, roughness, something more than memory, a hunger for the visible in his fingertips.

So they packed food and rolled their blankets and went searching for Joseph through Nazareth and all of Galilee. It was his voice Jesus heard, loud and boisterous, sitting at a table with other men, his back to the door.

"Weren't you the one who married that girl?" one man said, laughing, and others joined in. "You look like that man, but older." The room was dark, the men dejected.

"It wasn't me," Joseph said.

"You aren't the one whose wife 'saw an angel'?" another man laughed.

"I'm telling you," Joseph's voice rose, "it wasn't me." He glanced over his shoulder then and through the open door saw the back of his son.

Jesus walked away but John walked in.

14

A Colloquy

"HOW DID YOU know to go to Egypt?" John asked, pulling up a chair, touching Joseph on his forearm, the first of many questions.

"God used to speak to me in dreams," Joseph said. "Then I didn't want his dreams anymore."

Joseph often sat at the inn. He had papers and John saw that there were more jammed into his pocket. "I want a world like other men," his uncle said. "That first, before anything fancy's added on." He signaled the waiter. "This morning, for instance, I saw a bull being led to the Temple for sacrifice."

John immediately thought of the wide and detailed fan of the Law. The bull would have been a male without blemish, the sacrifice of a wealthy man, not a mere lamb or goat or turtledove. He would place his hands on the bull's head to recognize its innocence, that it would be killed in the man's place, to make atonement for him.

"So I drew the bull," Joseph said, bringing John back from his reverie. "I draw a lot lately."

"May I see?"

"I did a series. I'm trying to work something out." Joseph spread the papers out on the table.

But it was not what John expected. His uncle had not drawn an altar or the sons of Aaron taking the blood and sprinkling it. He hadn't drawn the priests skinning the bull, cutting it into pieces, laying down the wood, laying the parts onto the wood, the head and the fat in that order. He hadn't drawn the priest washing the legs of the bull or its entrails. Or the meal offerings of cereals and vegetables sacrificed in addition to the bull, their preparation, the wheat flour baked, fried or cooked in a pan, the dough with oil and salt but no honey or leaven. Joseph hadn't drawn the incense the wealthy man would bring.

"This was the first one," Joseph said, tapping it. Instead of the lush elaboration of the Law, John saw that his uncle was going in the opposite direction. Trying to find in the bull what was essential. To remove the rest. To see who he really is, John thought, in each drawing, the bull facing the same way, but more details removed than in the drawing before. Six drawings in all and the last, one simple curved line. And he admired what his uncle was doing and wanted to find a way to do the same thing.

As he headed home, John thought again of the laws of slaughter stipulated in Leviticus. He knew exactly how the bull had been treated, the many details to inflict as little pain as possible. That the slaughterer could not be a deaf-mute or a minor and must be of sound mind. That the knife must be perfectly smooth, tested on the flesh of the finger and then on the fingernail. That the flesh of the bull would not be consumed if pain had been inflicted in any of five ways: by delay or pressure or digging or slipping or tearing. The knife must move in a continuous forward and backward motion without interruption, the cut made gently without force, the knife drawn across the throat only and not inserted into the flesh, the cut made in the prescribed section of the neck so that the windpipe and gullet would not be dislocated.

These elaborations are signs of love, John thought, just as his uncle's drawings were signs of love and the press for understanding. And John sat on the side of the road and wept in anger at Herod for not giving to his father the courtesy and honor and compassion that was given, that morning, to the bull.

15

John the Forerunner
in the Wilderness

"WHY DON'T YOU go back to the wilderness?" Elizabeth offered, seeing the restlessness of her son. "God can be found in anger," she added, reading his heart. "He can be found everywhere." And in the spaciousness of his mother's words, John could feel both the intensity of his anger and his fondness for the mountain that had sheltered him and his mother and for the angel who had led them home.

SO JOHN WENT back to the desert's dryness, its allure, to the ant and the bumblebee and lion, to the snow leopard, the raven and the ram.

HE CRIED OUT to the wilderness, crying out for his father. And the wilderness answered saying, "I am he."

16

The Baptism of Jesus

JESUS WENT TO be baptized, to confess the sin of his being born. The pressure bore down, a past he could neither escape nor repair. "If it weren't for me," he told John often, "you'd still have a father." The wound bright, vivid and sparkling.

The villagers called him the crippled boy who carries his past on his shoulders like a house.

FROM A GREAT distance he heard John calling, "You breed of vipers!" in a voice fierce with certainty.

And Jesus told himself, John is right. I am a viper.

17

On the River Bank

TINY BIRDS WALKED at John's ankles, held by delicate gold chains, rumor being that the birds bound themselves to him. The bees gave him honey and the camel its coat. "You'll be like me someday," the camel had warned him. "They'll take your voice away. I'm saying this as a warning," then died. John skinned it with a knife, burned the carcass, wore the camel's hide and never ate flesh again. Until the locusts came and said, "Let us be the great exception," dying at his feet in great numbers and in his hair and beard and on his shoulders in swarms. He wrapped them in muslin and carried them in a pouch at his waist, eating the locusts, guaranteeing their distinction that way, as they had hoped. To not be forgotten, along with the honey.

To others John appeared exotic but to Jesus he looked only more himself, coalesced, purposeful, all else fallen away, the city, his mother's nobility, her fruit tartlets and his paper wings. John looked ancient and Jesus wondered if death brought this about, his father's early death, or if it was the wilderness.

JOHN SENSED HIS cousin was near and when Jesus stood before him with eyes full of sorrow and penance, John pulled away and refused the exact thing Jesus desired. "No," he said. "I won't."

The sky was quiet and the leaves on the trees shimmered nervously, waiting for a resolution, an eagle circled high above, eavesdropping, the sun sent its light equally onto both men, the waters up to their waist, the bystanders restless, until, at last, each spoke to the other.

"I've been waiting for you," John said. "I'm clearing your path." A dove landed in the branch overhead, carrying Heaven on its back, and a voice saying, "This is my beloved son in whom I am well pleased."

JESUS SAW THROUGH the water the long head of his cousin the prophet, he smelled his sour breath, his beard and matted hair, the honey caught at his lips, the flies buzzing near it, all the ways physical beauty was absent, and he shuddered, not because John lacked comeliness but because he saw the large, magnificent head of his cousin resting in a pool of blood.

John shuddered, too, greenish silt in the oiled curls of his cousin and he thought, you will soon be like me, little brother. My life has reached its purpose. And my end will be violent. I feel it in the wind. So will yours, my pretty little brother with your oiled curls and shopkeepers.

Faces inches apart, the sour breath of one mingling with the minted breath of the other, they stood a long while, silence clamping its arms around them, forming a room, a vault, and in that vault they both saw the jolting arrival of a completely new kind of time.

WHEN THE CROWDS had gone and dusk came, they sat beside each other on the riverbank and John said, "Now we know who we are."

"Today I am born," Jesus answered.

"I will perform no miracles," John told him, "but you, little cousin, will raise the dead."

18

Temptation

JESUS LEFT JOHN and went further into the wilderness where he stayed, in solitude and fasting, for forty days and forty nights, after which he was hungry. He heard from the wilderness in his heart, "If I am who John says I am, then this stone will become bread for me." He paced, circling the stone, his mouth watering, his stomach cramped into itself. But then rebuked that voice and headed out of the desert toward the city to buy bread, saying, "I will not be a magician."

At the cliff edge he saw the glory of the city below and before climbing down thought to test God by jumping from the cliff as if he could fly. But again he thought, I will not be a prophet like that.

Surveying the complexity of the city, he thought, if I leave this wilderness and go into the city people will flock to me and I will be greatest of the prophets. They will say that I am a god, surpassing even John. He explored the idea leisurely, admiring the details of it, a woman prostrate, an exultant following, zealous assistants. But then he stopped himself again, rebuking himself harshly because this was the hardest to resist, and said, "I will not bow down to my own vanity! I will not bow down to that throne, but will, instead, destroy it. I will be a servant."

In this way he sidestepped not only his vanity but also depression, and so laid down the burden of his life, for the fact of it, for the senseless shedding of innocent blood that had ensued, and only then did he feel ready to leave the wilderness and join, again, the company of men. Light, clear-headed and for the first time in his life, at peace, he offered prayers of thanksgiving. He removed his clothes and lay naked on the sand and rolled in it, front and back, pouring it onto his hair and feet, rubbing it onto his skin like a second baptism, a second birth, and covered in the dust of the sand, he rose and without cleaning it off, dressed again and descended the cliff. He saw a bride in the sky, her veil flowing from her head to her outstretched arms, her feet bound in white, and he knew she was the kingdom on its way, and knew that he would serve that kingdom and nothing else, her footsteps coming nearer and nearer, her perfume already alive in the dry desert air.

19

Jesus Calling His Disciples

PERHAPS HE THOUGHT he would find those bruised like himself, men and women who asked themselves similar questions, or those who also saw that figure in the sky, that kingdom on its way, and imminent.

Perhaps he was embarrassed often, flinging himself at others who looked away, disinterested, perplexed, or mocking. Perhaps he faltered, unskilled at reading what he saw in their eyes. "Leave your wife, your children and follow me." His invitation was harsh. "I am that knife blade, that severing force." It was an irrevocable demand and he was unable to soften it. The kingdom could demand all a person had, every comfort, every assumption. That narrow gate. Knowing that the narrow gate was not a metaphor.

Maybe in the end he stopped inviting others completely. He had twelve, which was not the fifty he'd hoped for, but it was something.

20

Wedding at Cana

IT WAS NEW and so welcome to feel peace, to have his life work laid out ahead with clarity, that it would be this and not that. So why now, he wondered, this question? He'd been home less than a week and already sensed that nauseating feeling of losing himself, that glide back into confusion and self-loathing. It angered him, her suggestion taking away what was so fragile, so that he ignored her and kept dancing, feverishly, in every line the men formed, carrying the groom on their shoulders. Right in the midst of this, gay and festive, he was angry, despite the tambourine and drum, feeling the abyss that lay between himself and his mother, himself and the world.

SHE HAD FELT agitated, as if an opportunity was announcing itself, an opening. Dance after dance she watched her son, glad to see him capable of happiness, but the pressure inside kept rising, demanding an action.

Then he saw something compelling in her expression, asking a question as if it were, or could become, his question, putting herself again at a precipice, at the edge of understanding, so that he stopped dancing and drew near. By the time he stood breathless at her table, she was able to say with confidence, "Take this risk." The belly dancer assumed the floor, the guests returned to their tables, and he left behind the very clarity that had given him peace.

WET BURLAP WAS draped over the fruits and sliced meats to keep them cool. The kitchen smelled of oven-baked aubergine, oil beads on the vine leaves stuffed with rice and herbs, the tart fragrance of vinegar, pickled cucumbers and chilies, lamb sausages splattered on the grill, the hearty smell of fava bean croquettes, his favorite, it was voluptuous and overpowering against the force of his concentration, waiters bustling past with trays held high on their fingertips.

He sat on the floor in the dark back hall, the water jars in a stately row. Just beyond the shade, a lizard watched from his hot stone.

SOMETHING was ratified.

HE DID NOT return to the dance floor but remained at the side when the first cup was poured. The groom cheered, his surprise and pleasure, and across the room, his mother stared at him, wiping her eyes.

THEY DIDN'T SPEAK while walking home. A future lay beyond the darkness of his life, a foreign landscape he could see now, with pines and snow and brittle light.

IN PART, SHE wished she'd been wrong. If her son could change water into wine, what else would come? She wondered where Joseph was just then.

"If he is a prophet," she could say to him if he were there, "he will die a prophet. He will be hated by many who danced with him today."

She missed Joseph, missed what was good between them, what had been good, and wondered, what will become of this dancer, our son?

21

The Woman with
an Issue of Blood

T HE WORDS OF the Law came to her with the dawn light just
as they had for twelve years without ceasing, in her sleep
and waking so that being "unclean" eclipsed everything else she
knew about herself—her facial features, her hair color, the sound
of her laugh, the shape of her thigh, the names of her cousins, her
favorite bread, the words to songs she was taught as a child. The
constant flow of blood eclipsed her hopes for marriage, a family, travel, and eventually even visitors. With luck, her education
was one thing preserved because she could read and could ask her
neighbor, a scholar of some merit, to lend her books, which he did,
being Greek, not a Hebrew, and unafraid of her condition.

Her neck, arms, feet, breasts, all unclean, whatever she touched,
even clothing, also unclean.

*"If a woman have an issue of blood many days beyond the days
of her separation, she shall be unclean. Every bed she lies upon shall*

be unclean, whatsoever she sits upon. Whosoever touches these
things shall be unclean and shall wash himself and his clothes. . . ."

A visitor would have to bathe and wash all of her own clothes
afterward even though, to prepare, the woman with the issue of
blood washed her floors, her table, and sheets.

At first neighbors had visited her with regularity, the blood
draining away her strength, and they could see this. They rotated
the chores among themselves, the constant rinsing of the rags in
cold water, then boiling them, hanging them to dry then fold-
ing. The bed sheets, the blankets, all of the furniture washed, not
because blood had touched it but because the woman had.

Eventually she removed all fabric, the cushion from her chair,
the tablecloths, the curtains, the bedding, so that she slept on wood,
sat on wood, ate on wood, and in this way saved energy, which
was the focus of her mind, how to battle the deadening fatigue.

In those first days the women agreed among themselves to
make an exception to custom and trained not only their daughters
but also their sons to help, to haul the copious supply of water for
rinsing, washing, rinsing again. Young sons, seven years old and
up, were eager, created teams, named themselves Badger, Owl,
Rat. They set jars of water outside her door, knocked, ran away.
She lifted them in, returned them to the mat empty. For a few
years she set out with the empty jars cards, cookies, sweets. Then
just notes.

The women visited when she had the bare wood then not at all
and the sons and daughters tired of the job and drifted away one
by one. She hired strangers but the constant visits to the doctors,

all to no avail, left her penniless with neither companionship nor cure. Her life had become a circular pattern of the body moving in space, to the basin, the stove, to the walls, the bed for rest, back to the basin, the stove, the walls again.

A handyman from Galilee, new to the village, built her wood drying racks that attached to the walls and could fold back against them when empty. The rags hung in straight white rows. "You'll entertain again," he said, nailing the last one, but, knowing this wasn't true, she only weakened and grew scared.

WHEN NEWS CAME that a prophet was healing others, she went to see him and in the dense crowd, reached to touch the back hem of his robe. Right away she felt the flow of blood stop and some of her energy return. The cure was complete and instantaneous, which caused Jesus to turn in her direction and say, to no one in particular, "Something just left me."

The disciples murmured first that such a woman had come into the press of the crowd. Then some heard Jesus say to her, "Your faith has made you whole," but faith in what? they wondered. She hadn't professed any faith, hadn't said anything at all, not even his name. "He's going to her house," they murmured, shaking their heads.

"I KNOW THE rules," she assured him once they sat down on the two wooden chairs at her small square table, its short, rough planks. She mentioned Leviticus, chapter 15. "Noble and solemn," she granted, "but not perfect."

"You didn't repent, yet you were healed," Jesus said.

"I was."

She felt again how personal it was to discuss matters of the body. That her body felt personal to her again was another healing. "I didn't feel contrite. I felt ill and tired," she explained.

She offered and he accepted a cup of tea.

"You have great power," she continued, setting down the cup. "Perhaps instead of feeling it leave, you could learn to release it intentionally. Maybe it can be gathered and aimed."

"I didn't even touch you. Yet something crossed that gap."

"Like love does," she said.

It was nice to see him take the tea and put it to his mouth. To drink from it without hesitating.

"WHAT DO YOU believe in?" he asked her.

"The empirical."

She poured herself a second cup.

"You said you went to many physicians and none healed you."

"If they were good physicians, they would have. The body is a kingdom," she said, "with laws of its own. What they offered me didn't help because they hadn't studied this kingdom," she touched her chest.

"So you came to me."

"I was desperate."

"And you received a miracle," he said a second time.

"I did."

At this they both stopped.

"AND I'M GRATEFUL for it," she began again. "But I also want to study the natural world, to better see when nature is superseded, to better see the miraculous when it occurs. I want that differentiation. I read the Scriptures. But I've also read Hippocrates."

He lifted his cup to toast her.

"You can do something about this. If you change the language you'll change perception. Contagion is not a moral issue. It's a matter of hygiene." As she spoke, Jesus saw her whole body become young and centered and pensive, her feet grew large as if grounding her vision on the earth, her hands large also. The house no longer smelled of blood, but of mint, parsley and cinnamon. "The study of the body could also be a form of faith," she speculated. "To address the body on its own could be a religious act." Here he smiled.

She told him she often heard terms she did not know: autopsy, dissection, sterilization, isolation, vaccination, anesthesia, airborne pathogens. In her visions she saw the study of blood, organs, fluids of all kinds, and saw new jobs with new names like "surgeon," "nurse," and "infectious disease specialist." Others followed after Hippocrates. Galen, Lister, Pasteur, Charcot, Paré, Fractastorius, Nightingale.

She told him she'd named this vision that would save others like herself, "Medicine, the Beautiful Science."

And Jesus said, "It's the future."

At this, she wept.

22

The Woman with
an Issue of Blood, II

L OOKING AT THE rags on the drying racks, she realized she
would fold them into neat piles and give them to the poor.
A joyful act.

WHEN JESUS STOOD to leave she paused. A daydream came in
which people clipped strands of his hair and fingernails from his
body, cut swatches from what he wore. The robe that she'd touched
had been plain linen, but in her daydream it was embroidered and
trimmed with jewels. That door through which something more
than nature had come.

"HERE, TAKE ONE," she pressed one of the folded clean rags into
his palm. "White," she said, "the color of your resurrection."

This troubled him. Not because it was a completely new idea, but because it was an idea he hadn't shared with anyone, not even John, the disciple whom he most loved.

23

Legion

J ESUS AND HIS disciples crossed the sea and when they landed
came upon a man who dwelled among the tombs, so fierce he
broke through the chains and fetters by which he was bound. He
cut himself with stone, and no man could tame him.

"Don't torment me!" he screamed, seeing Jesus.

"What is your name?"

"Don't send me into the swine!"

"Tell me, what is your name?"

"Legion," the man said, "because we are many."

REMEMBERING THE WOMAN with the issue of blood, Jesus
gathered the power that was his and aimed it at the ferocity of
Legion, ordering the spirits that tormented him into the swine
nearby, a herd of about two thousand, who ran down the cliff
and into the sea.

Astonished, the swineherds fled to the city and told what they
had seen and when the people saw that the man they called "the

maniac" was sitting and clothed and in his right mind they were afraid and begged Jesus to depart from their coasts.

But Jesus refused.

"Those are all me," Legion said when he saw the swine bobbing in the water.

FOR DAYS JESUS watched Legion haul the carcasses up the cliff, two on each shoulder, slapping the bodies down onto the grass. "They're smart animals," he told Jesus. "Did you have to do it that way?"

Again and again Legion climbed down the cliff and returned. He buried each in a grave, intentionally dug shallow so that the mounds could be seen all at once. "I want to see all the parts of myself," he explained. He buried them in a grid. "Because they belong together," he said.

And Jesus saw how violent healing could be. How easy it was to be violent. And he decided to resist violence when it came to him and to not inflict any. He vowed to never again heal a person in that way. And he repented for the violence with which he had healed Legion.

"TELL ME WHAT happened," he said.

Legion tried to explain, but as he spoke he became agitated and could no longer sit peacefully. "Today is flaring up," he said, "today is flaring up!"

"What do you mean?"

"I see a bloodstained toad instead of my white kitten." He paced back and forth. "God has gone away!" Then he ran. "Love is punctured!"

LEGION RAN BETWEEN the tombs, yelling, crashing into Jesus, running again, between the headstones and monuments, slapping his hands against them, scraping his hands on the cement, marble, stone, until they bled. His palms bloody from the stones then running away again. Dried blood on the headstones, new red blood dripping down the sides.

Sometimes he ran until nightfall while Jesus stood in the posture of *orans*, hands lifted to the sky, to express the immutability of what he was witnessing, that ancient gesture of prayer. Each time he returned, Jesus held Legion. He'd watched him, had not taken his eyes off him as he ran.

"Not once?" Legion asked, once he calmed.

"Not once," Jesus said, weeping.

TOUCHING ONE OF the scars where Legion had cut himself with a stone, Jesus saw, on the insides of each forearm, scars white from age, a lattice of fine lines intersecting like a mesh.

"Let me see all of them," Jesus asked carefully, and, standing, Legion removed his shirt. His chest and shoulders and arms were cross-hatched with scars like threads.

"Are there more?"

Legion turned away, sure that Jesus would leave him if he saw his legs and back. But instead he heard that Jesus was very close. He heard that he was crying.

"No one has ever wept with me before."

"Maybe the swine did," Jesus offered.

"I WOULD LIKE to see all of them, if you're willing," he said.

So Legion took off his sandals and showed the network of scars on the soles of his feet. Then he dropped his pants. The scars were dense on his buttocks, his thighs and calves, his lower back, the web of raised white lines so thorough that Legion's skin was barely visible, as if clothed in white lace, white socks, white gloves, white stockings, white pants. At his groin his skin was solid white, as if buried under a fall of snow.

He carefully dressed again, smoothed his hair, his beard, tipped his head to one side then the other, the pop sound of tension released, and fell silent.

Jesus could not believe how much cruelty could come to one child and again he repented for the violence with which he had healed Legion.

"I WANT TO go with you," Legion said on the forty-first day when all that needed to be spoken was spoken, and all that needed to be shown.

"You can't," Jesus answered.

"Please!" Legion implored him.

"If you follow me, you will suffer. You've suffered enough already." Then he picked up his satchel and threw it over his shoulder. "Tell your story to others. The bad parts and the good. It will help them. And besides, you don't need me anymore. You have all of yourself now."

Legion handed Jesus his sharpened stones, the edges like blades, one by one so that later when Jesus boarded the boat his pockets were heavy with them.

"Keep one," he gave one back to Legion. "Don't be afraid of it. It's a sign of your victory."

LEGION SLAPPED HIS chest. "Don't overlook the body when you go about your father's business," he smiled. "Don't forget about touch." And then they hugged.

Jesus headed down the coast to where the ship was anchored and turning back, saw Legion on the top of the cliff having followed him the three miles.

IN TIME LEGION left the cemetery. He left his field of mounds and then he left Judah altogether. He went to a country where he was not known, married, and had seven sons. He continued to be called Legion because he was rich with offspring and he loved them as he wanted to have been loved by his parents, with exceeding tenderness. When he spoke of what happened to him in the field, men and women marveled.

MANY TIMES JESUS thought of Legion and their time together. When he rebuked the scribes and the Pharisees for their hypocrisy he compared them to white sepulchers and then saw again in his mind's eye Legion running through the night, moonlight on his scars and body whiter than in the sun.

"Suffer the children to come to me," he taught the disciples later, also remembering Legion and all he had overcome. How he had carried the parts of himself inside, alive and waiting to be joined. That those were young voices, held in his body, scared but fierce and obstinate, the chains that could not bind Legion, the fetters that he broke through. That it was those young, desperate voices who first called him "the Christ."

WHEN HIS SONS had grown and married, Legion returned to the coast, to the grid of green mounds, and with the sharp stone carved his tombstone, leaving instructions with the new herdsmen to bury him in the green grid along with the swine. The tombstone read,

> "Here lies Legion, being one man
> who was once many.
> Before the Christ came."

24

Joseph Visiting

K NOWING THAT JESUS was now a young man, Joseph came home bringing hand tools in a leather apron to give to his son, along with small samples of different woods, myrtle, pear wood, sycamore. But Jesus was nowhere to be found and Joseph kept the tools under the table without mentioning them and took them when he left.

MARY TOLD HIM of the miracles Jesus was performing, the wedding at Cana, the woman with an issue of blood, a man named Legion. But when she slipped and spoke of their son's "heavenly father," Joseph regretted coming home. Seeing his sadness, she quickly added, "You've shown him what a good father is, too."

He remembered that consoling is a part of friendship, so that perhaps they had become friends after all. He appreciated her effort, hugged her on the step and felt a momentary desire to be with her again. In the small things, she could sometimes be wonderful. If he could just have the small things, these acts of kindness and not all the rest. If he could have these small moments without the constant sense that God should have chosen a better man, then he could have stayed.

She asked if he still had dreams and he said, "Yes, but of different things." Had he summoned the courage he would have told her he liked to draw the dreams that came. Sunlight falling on roofs, colonnades. Last night he'd dreamt of a different kind of monument, years in the future, twenty centuries at least. It was a place where memory was preserved but there was no Mercy Seat, no animals were led there for slaughter, bull or turtledove. It had a grove of locust trees planted in the sky, like a world turned upside down. And he drew that monument. Light falling on that form that spoke of the great absence of God.

25

The Man Blind from Birth

WHEN JESUS PASSED by a man blind from birth, his disciples asked if the man's condition was because of his own sins or the sins of his parents, and Jesus, remembering the woman with the issue of blood, said solemnly, "Neither."

He sat down next to the man, the two of them whispering to each other in the chamber of their bodies, shutting out all others, even the heat. "You can use this," the man said, tapping the ground, because he often packed it on his cheeks and neck, letting the clay dry to a mask then peeling it off, which made him feel clean.

Jesus spat and made clay of his spittle and focused his intention, remembering the power he possessed, to use it wisely. He anointed the man's eyes with the clay and touched his face tenderly because of Legion, and felt the energy flow out to the blind man through his hands.

"Go wash in the pool of Siloam," he instructed and the man went and washed in the pool and received sight.

NOW THE MAN was questioned by his neighbors how his eyes were opened, and he told them what Jesus had done. When asked where Jesus was, the man said he didn't know and he repeated the same to the Pharisees. They then called his parents who answered only that, indeed, the man was their son and he was born blind. They added, "But we do not know how he sees," distancing themselves from him. When pressed further, they said, "He is of age, ask him," and again, "He shall speak for himself," never adding that their son was reliable or trustworthy or that he was not prone to exaggeration, which hurt him.

BEING BLIND ALL of his life, he was a careful listener and careful in his speech so that when he was brought a second time before the Pharisees he was clear about what he knew and what he did not know. Asked whether Jesus was a sinner, he did not know, and stated simply, "I was blind and now I see," clinging to that certainty.

IN THE DAYS that followed, he saw that his parents did not love him. He told himself, this is the price of healing, the price of sight. He saw that they did not love him as they loved themselves and remembered that Jesus had asked him three times if he was sure he wanted to see, saying, "Blindness can be a blessing."

In the hovel of his parents' home, he saw what he had often smelled, that it was dirty and disorganized, everything in disrepair. He saw that his father feared his mother, which he'd sensed from a young age, but had not known, until seeing, the tension and fear that marked his father's face with rivulets where anger gathered and ran down.

DAILY, HE DREW water from the well, helping his mother, cleaning the house, washing the clothes, the fresh water for drinking. The women and the young girls and boys learned to hesitate, some even learned patience, as he waited for the water's surface to settle into glass so that he could hold his face over it, staring a long time at his reflection, no matter how recently he had done it, seeing a stranger there.

He saw his thick black lashes and brows, the scar on his cheek. He saw that he was fair and to his own eyes beautiful, so that he changed his name from the One Blind from Birth to The Believer. And they called it The Believer's Well, the Well of the Disciple.

THE BELIEVER LIVED with his parents and cared for them into their old age. He also followed Jesus from a distance, doing small practical things, helping secure the room for the last meal, finding the donkey.

"I came to bring division" is what Jesus had been preaching, the cutting in of the future and of judgment, the cost of doing the will of God, the closeness of the end times that he and his cousin John both felt, that urgency. But seeing that the man lived peaceably with his parents who did not really love him, Jesus learned that sometimes doing God's will was gentle and easy and that discipleship could lead to harmony instead of division. A low gate, he thought, not always a knife blade.

When the crowd of five thousand listening to Jesus grew hungry, it was The Believer who suggested a few loaves and a few fish could feed them all. "The loaves will multiply the way love does," he told Jesus. "Exponentially."

26

Elizabeth's Dream

ELIZABETH SAW A bowl with a lid rolling down behind her and woke shaking. She reached across the bed for Zachariah, forgetting again that he wasn't there, for years forgetting this. Inside the lidded bowl, the head of someone she knew.

Was it Zachariah? But no, he'd been murdered with a sword to the heart. The neighbors had answered as best they could. By the time news of his death reached the holy mountain where she and John were sheltered, by the time they were able to walk back, days had passed and her husband's body was already buried. She'd fled to him, knew that a horse was needed, a mule, her feet sore, her legs giving out. She'd believed her neighbors, too swallowed in grief of their own to hold onto anything but what they'd seen. No, it was not her noble husband.

She pushed herself up to better see back into the dream and her breath gave way. Her arms grew cold and she knew that the head in the bowl was that of her son.

27

The Martyrdom of John
the Forerunner

J ESUS SENT HIS disciples to ask for the body of John but they
were given the body only and Jesus wept seeing the ragged
neck. He wanted that rough, angry voice more than anything else,
that mouth.

He and Elizabeth sat on the low chairs without speaking for
seven days and neither left the house. He did not go to the house of
Mary and Martha even though word came that Lazarus, whom he
loved, was gravely ill. He looked at the toys in John's room, string,
crayons, paper wings, and felt again how much the world hates
innocence. He remembered on the banks of the Jordan, as they
parted, John had said, "They'll kill me and you, too, dear cousin.
I'll perform no miracles, but you will raise the dead."

28

Lazarus

J ESUS LISTENED TO John, the disciple whom he most loved.
"Do you think you can do it?"

"I'm not sure."

"You let him die."

"I did."

"If you raise him from the dead, they will kill you."

WHEN LAZARUS APPEARED, Jesus looked at the crowd and at his disciples and thought, one of you will betray me.

Seeing Jesus' face, John turned away, saying, "Now you've gone too far."

29

Mary Magdalen

FOR THREE DAYS Mary's mother had refused to bury her husband. She'd resisted all the habits of burial, making enemies of her friends due to what seemed to them a lack of piety. But to her it was piety. "The Lord would never leave me alone with six children!" she'd said, watching the body, sure that God would bring her husband back to life.

Mary had joined her mother, prayed for her father's return, and when it didn't happen her mother grew angry. Then she grew sullen and bitter and never again visited the house of the Lord.

On the fourth day she announced, "I keep the Sabbath holy by blaspheming," brash and unafraid. "I keep the Sabbath holy by taking men into my bed and you will, too." She fit her daughter with jewelry on her neck and ears, plaiting her hair, and on the fifth day she sent Mary into the streets of Magdala.

"THEY COME HERE for only one thing," her mother's instructions began. "Don't make friends. Don't think you are special no matter

how often a man returns, no matter how often he says he will leave
his wife. They all make promises, they can't help it. There is only
one reason a man comes here and when you give it to him, they
leave." Then she added, "Always take the money first. Count it.
And bring it to me."

In this way Mary and her mother fed the boys in the family
until they were grown.

Her mother hired other girls. Local ones, foreigners, tall and
short, heavy and thin. "For spice," she said. "Never be boring.
Wash yourself. Read. Have things to talk about. Sometimes they
just want to talk. But mostly, especially the young ones, they come
here for just one thing."

AND SO IT began. The brothel flourished and Mary forgot about
the love she felt as a child for her father. Forgot what it felt like to
love and to be loved, to run toward another who waits.

The narrow dirt corridor between the rooms, the hand broom
she used to sweep off the sheet, the basin under the bed, the green
twigs she lit between customers, bringing them to the doorway, the
threshold, to purify it, and then stepping outside onto the door-
mat, lifting one foot, holding the flame under it, then the other, for
cleansing. Checking for sores and bruises.

MARY HEARD OF the raising of Lazarus, heard of threats to the
prophet's life, that he might soon be arrested, and she wanted to
meet him while there was still time. "All good men go away," she
told herself but went out in daylight to find him, nonetheless.

Older, being thirty-eight to his thirty-three years, she could see in his eyes that he wanted wisdom in a hurry. She said she had nothing to give, nothing to offer. "But you do," he protested.

She felt most comfortable with men sure to leave. Married men. Soldiers. Even, once, an old man near death. She had, since thirteen, learned to not mourn, to brush her hair afterward, to clean her teeth. "I know how to get past love. I'm older than you are. I've had many." But Jesus argued with her, saying, "That's not true."

"YOU'LL JUST GET hurt," her mother warned, seeing that she was nervous each time they met. She knew he didn't want what other men sought in her yet she found herself fearing he wouldn't return because, with him, she remembered her father and felt again that wound.

It was her childlike quality Jesus found attractive. That she was tough but also fragile. They made a game of it, Jesus hiding his face behind his hands then popping out, saying, "Hah!" which startled her every single time because, somehow, she thought once gone, gone forever. It startled her even when he did it five times in a row. "I'm coming back," he told her each time they parted. "You'll see."

"ON THE THIRD day I'm going to rise from the dead," he said near the end, which angered her because it was specific and he seemed so convinced of it.

"Of course you are," she humored him. She'd encountered men with wild visions before. One would be an emperor, another, a general. This was part of her job, to hold these daydreams as if they could happen. It was a form of play, almost sexual, like costumes and masks, whips and ankle cuffs. She obliged men this way as a courtesy, to keep them coming back, and had long ago mastered the expression of seriousness.

But Jesus was not a customer. They were friends. And she loved him. "Don't say that," she rebuked him. She wanted his leaving, if he must leave, to take a simpler form. Without the fantasies, the outlandishness. "I like everything about you but your false promises," she chided. But then she grew anxious and softened, that this might really be true, and said, "If it's going to happen as you say, give your mother to John. He will be good to her."

JESUS TOOK HER to the river where he and his mother had buried the myrrh. When they walked through the streets men whistled, women turned away and looked down hissing until she passed. He was talking about his death all the time then. Since Lazarus.

"Bury my body," he said. "Put me someplace. In a grave. Promise me!"

They dug in the mud for the jar. On her knees, her dress dampened, dirt in her fingernails.

"Where did you get this?" she wiped off the jar, lifted the lid. "It's very costly."

"Use it on me," he said, "when the time comes. Remember me," he said.

"You're always asking me to do that."

"When you eat bread think of me. Think of me when you drink from a cup. I mean this," he pleaded.

"I will remember you, my prince, for the rest of my life."

30

John the Beloved

"YOUR END IS coming," John, the beardless one, said. It was painful, holding all of John's sweetness one last time. "I'm going to prepare a place for you, John." Seeing that he would be the only Apostle to live into old age, the only one not to be killed for his sake, Jesus then whispered, "Time will be tender toward you."

But John wept and wanted none of this.

"Hold me!" he demanded and could not be consoled.

31

The Last Supper/Remember Me

"I T'S TIME," JESUS said, feeling that his arrest was near, going to the room The Believer had found for them to share the Passover meal. A rented room where no one felt at home. Splinters in the skin, makeshift arrangements. He needed discomfort as he began to loosen himself, loosen his body, to break himself as if into pieces to be fed to strangers and dogs. His body that didn't want to turn from the world, custard on the tongue, the love of his family and followers like fragrant leaves.

JUDAS LUNGED FOR the pitcher of water. O God! Purify!

Watching him Jesus thought, now the wheel is turning. Judas fled the room.

HE SAID TO the others, "This meal will be our last."

Taking some bread he said, "This is what will happen to my body," and tore it into pieces.

"When you eat it," he pleaded, "remember me."

32

Veronica

No one else had seen the dove descend over the head of Jesus then fly away or heard the voice that came from the sky saying, "This is my beloved son, in whom I am well-pleased," except the young woman in line with her mother, bored and distracted, who looked away from the River Jordan and into the tree. She'd rolled her eyes when she heard it and thought, not everyone wants the supernatural.

Taking wide strides, she walked through the crowd to the dye shop. Clean white cotton squares in her pockets, she and her mother would select the right color for her special dress. Crimson? Violet? They would dye the corners, make samples, take them home. In four weeks her boyfriend would return from the Roman Army, conscripted when they were in sweet time.

Through the commotion on the street, she saw another condemned man, another cross. Executions had become common, which annoyed her. But this man staggered and she felt sorry for him, sweat like blood falling from his face. "Be careful!" her mother cautioned as she moved closer toward him. Her mother not wanting to be seen in public so close to a criminal. Her husband, a traitor, having been buried outside the walls, and they still lived in the shadow of his shame.

A soldier whistled, jibed at her beauty. Used to such attention, she gestured obscenely back.

"We're late!" her mother scolded, pulling at her daughter's arm, but the young woman then recognized the man, suffering under the weight of the cross he could barely manage, and, taking one of the rags, she put it against his face then whispered, "I was at the Jordan. I heard that voice. I saw that bird in the tree."

THE DYE WOMAN had pigments boiling in pots. One by one, they dipped the rags in, stirring with a stick. Before dropping it in, the daughter gasped, stuffed the rag quickly into her pocket, excused herself and ran to the backyard where the dye woman's children played. She opened the cloth against her leg. It wasn't how she'd seen him, sorrowful and bruised. Instead it was the face of a victor. A band of blue and one of orange framed his face. She rubbed the cloth on a stone, the children laughed at her, watched, then returned to their game, but the image was still there.

The next day she took it to her father's grave, laid it open, hoping the full-day sun would bleach out the face, but nothing altered.

Returning home, she saw her mother running out to meet her, waving her arms, calling her name. There was bad news. Her boyfriend had been killed. His hand returned, cut off at the wrist.

"Come back!" her mother screamed, but the young woman ran out again past the city gate all the way to the death hill. The criminal whom she'd touched was hanging there between two others.

"It's not your face I want!" she threw the rag down, stomped it into the sand with her foot. "I don't want your face! I want his!"

WOMEN CARRIED HER home. One picked up the rag blown against the stone and fell silent, folded it into her sleeve. In low tones, she spoke solemnly to the young woman's mother. "We must rename this girl." She showed the cloth. "From now on we must call her Veronica," and then explained "verus," meaning "true," and "iconicus," meaning "image."

"My daughter? 'True-Image'?" And then she saw the face on the cloth.

They mounted it under glass set about with precious stones, candles, flowers, and herbs. Pilgrims came. They called it a holy visage, gave it titles, "The Icon of the Lord on the Cloth," "The Not-Made-with-Hands," the "Vericle."

VERONICA THOUGHT, THIS has nothing to do with me.

She did not want a miracle. She wanted her boyfriend to have found her beautiful in her bridal dress.

33

The Place of the Skull

WHEN THE SOLDIER thrust his sword into Jesus' side and water and blood flowed down, Mary reached to bind the body whole again. But the soldier blocked her and she fell in a swoon, not because she was unprepared for grief but because she had seen it coming for over thirty years and had found no way to stop it.

John held her and as she fell she thought, looking at the soldier, you made this wound for me, so that I can put all my suffering into the cave of his body, still alive, still warm. O wound! O Holy Door!

34

Joseph at Golgatha

JOSEPH CROUCHED BEHIND a bush and heard words as they moved between the bodies in front of him like a sieve, sifted to brief sentences. "Forgive them, Father, for they know not what they do." And, "Today you will be with me in Paradise." And so it went, words trickling back to him through the crowd, then through the tiny leaves of the bush, the thin, brittle branches, then past the little red birds busy at his face.

When he came out from behind the bush and stood, he saw his son and thought, he is saving himself, healing himself of all his sorrows.

From his hands and feet, that last drop of blood.

35

Mary Magdalen at Golgotha

MARY DREW NEAR the cross and again thought, the erotic and the spiritual are one hunger.

She drew closer and heard, "Your father died and your mother turned you out. But, Mary, look at me and see. It isn't true that you were never loved."

36

God

J ESUS CRIED OUT to his father, "Why have you forsaken me?"
And God said to the underworld, "Take him, he's yours."
Hearing this, Jesus breathed his last.

GOD HID BEHIND the sun, saying, "It is true, then. I am not
merciful."

37

Joseph of Arimathea

IN HIS AWKWARDNESS, as he took the body down, Joseph of
Arimathea was struck by the chaos of mercy and the swiftness
of revenge.

THE CROWD THINNED and Joseph, the father of Jesus, noticed a
woman with long brown hair standing off to the side, weeping yet
resolute, middle-aged yet graceful, her posture carrying a message
of courage. The sun was well behind the hill and the tiny red birds
hushed for the night. He had seen his wife collapse, fall to her left,
a young man holding her. He saw them finally walk away.

He wondered if he could have, after all, stayed with the boy and
his mother, if they could have found a way to surmount all that life
had dealt them. Wondered why, when he'd loved his wife and she
had loved him, it became something else, a third body that lived
with and between them, so alive and grasping it was finally all that
felt real, while love, as a dream, was reeled back from the sky like
a kite brought down to a wide windowsill, the ball of twine getting

larger, string, the torn paper, all the mess of it on the sill, and then the dream of love contracting further to the size of a nutshell, round and wrinkled and hard, so small that he could hold it in the palm of his hand.

HE WATCHED HIS son, everyone gone but the tall resolute woman, and then a man he did not know, old and weary, balancing on a short ladder, who took the full weight of his son's body onto his shoulder like a net heavy with fish. He envied the man yet walked forward to assist.

"Did you know him?" the stranger asked him before leaving with the body.

It was a source of shame to watch the stranger take away the body of his only son, to a burial place already secured. To have assistants. To have a burial spot that was his own. Joseph had wanted that, too, a life that could be planned, supplied. It never seemed to be that way for him or for what had been their family and for this he had no way to account, doing his best to stick with what had occurred, to look straight ahead at life. But that never worked either, that straight-ahead look, because it could never take everything in.

He turned away from the scene, the soldiers dismantling the cross, the body of his son now gone, all three bodies gone, even the resolute woman with her long brown hair gone, and he put the nutshell into the pocket of his coat and walked home.

38

Legion, II

H E WAS THE first to sense it. He heard voices shouting, "Deliverer!" and "Savior!" and thought of the Christ.

He is freeing the chained, the fettered, the ones who've waited, Legion thought. Like he freed me.

39

The Descent into Hell

A S THEY BURIED Jesus in the tomb, God imagined an earlier world, with just the land and sea and heavens and plants, the creatures that had no heart at all. He wondered if he should return things to that state, abandon his project entirely, that long hope.

But he still wanted what he'd always most wanted, which was to be loved not for his power or his omniscience but for his mercy. And for that, he needed man. The ferns could never know his mercy or be grateful for it. The ferns could never love him or turn away from him as they could turn toward and away from the sun.

Then he thought, perhaps a revision is in order, and told himself, I should learn to do this to myself, to not need man. Wouldn't that be almost as good? A paler pleasure but not nothing.

AS THE SOLDIERS arrived to guard the tomb in which Jesus lay, God opened the drawer of the past and then lifted the veil of the future so that he could see, in one glance, all of time, from its beginning to its end, from what existed before time to what would exist after it, and he held time and all that it contained on his lap, and touched it and turned it over the way a grandparent holds a grandchild and so holds also the parents of the child, past and future, in an inspecting reverence. God held all of time together, and, seeing that he was alone and would cause harm to no one, he let himself feel all of the anger he saw in time, all of his fury, his disappointment at the floundering of man, at the cruelty and arrogance and pride and greed of man.

GOD HELD ALL of it in his hands and then, from deep within himself, forgave all of it, both in advance and in retrospect, so that his anger and his mercy together poured out like an envelope cut open. And the earth quaked and some of the dead rose from their tombs and the veil of the Temple was torn in two and when his mercy had consumed all of his anger God cried out, "It is finished!"

WHEN HE OPENED his eyes, God saw a procession without end, Eve at the front, the mother of mankind, all the prophets and holy men and women and children of all times and places, and people he did not know or could not remember. "Rescue us," he heard them say, "we have been waiting for you." And God saw Noah and then all those he'd slain. That each was waiting for him. That each had forgiven him. And because he had fashioned them in his own image, he saw that then he, too, must be merciful after all.

As he watched the long pageant, God saw not only the fact of his mercy but the extent of it. That not one was left in Hell, not one refused to forgive him, even Judas, not one.

And God wept at the beauty of their mercy, which was also his. His great mercy, *magnam misericordiam.* That it was infinite.

40

Mary Magdalen
at the Sepulchre

S HE'D COME TO see him one last time. To lift the linen nap-
kin from his face, to part his lips, to trace her finger along the
cracked tooth, the one in front, to press his tongue into submis-
sion. She'd wanted to say, "You were good to me." But his body
was not there, though the burial clothes were and they retained
the same bound shape, the body removed from them in some
inexplicable way. Because even his body was gone, she thought,
it's always like this, even after dying. A person leaves then takes
even more.

Unable to touch his body, she lifted the burial clothes to her
face. It didn't surprise her that they smelled of myrrh. The other
women brought spices and she brought the myrrh and they had
anointed him in death, raising his arms over his head as he lay
between them, rubbing myrrh and balsam onto his wrists and forearms, the silky brown hairs in the pit of his arms.

But the cloth now also held the sour smell of his perspiration, both metallic and nutty, she was sure of it. As if he'd worked to free himself, to slip through the fabric without disturbing it. As if the body had not been stolen. As if he'd struggled for his own release, which was a fantasy, and she stopped herself from going further with it, stopped herself from dreaming the impossible, as if he were alive and so would come back. She stopped herself from the empty foolishness of her mother.

Instead, she took the square cloth they'd used to cover his face and folded it in half then in half again and set it apart from the rest to say, "I, Mary the Magdalen was here. You loved me. When you were with me, you were different than all the others."

But then she remembered his words and, counting, knew it was now the third day. And, at this, her hands shook.

41

Mary Magdalen, Penitent

AFTER IT HAPPENED she fled to the desert, cut off her hair and spent her nights staring at the candle's single wick in penance, not because she'd been with many men but because she hadn't been able to imagine that he would come back. "I came to you first," he told her when she recognized him in the garden. "*Noli me tangere,*" he cautioned. Don't touch me. Not yet.

She gathered small bones, skeletons, the triangular skull of a garter snake, the thighbone of a squirrel, reminding herself that death is real. But love is stronger. Trying to enter that one thing. The blood that came down so precisely from his palm.

They called her Mother of Penitents and The First Witness to the Resurrection.

42

Zaccheus

S HE HAD COME to see if Jesus was remembered, as he had so
deeply wanted.

He looked down and saw a woman with cropped brown hair
holding small bones, the skull of a snake, a bird wing, leaning on a
cane. "Will you tell me about your afternoon with him?" she asked
and Zaccheus spoke to her, saying,

"WE ATE AT my table, oranges, olives." His voice was slow,
infused with a reverie and sadness, as if, for many years, he had
wanted to tell this story to someone. "He wasn't what I expected,"
he said then paused. "I could see that he didn't need me. He didn't
need me to change.

"Sandwiches and fruit," he continued, each word a break from
silence. "He told me, 'There's nothing wrong with your body,
Zaccheus,' when I saw my shadow on the dirt. He said, 'See how
whole it is?' And I thought maybe he was saying, 'You can stop
feeling like a failure now. You can stop feeling like a failure at love.'

"Then night fell and the profile of the hill became clear and harsh and then disappeared. I felt lost again, aswim. My body without circumference, without edge.

"'Go back to your tree, Zaccheus,' he said before he left me. 'It will be paradise for you. Happiness isn't here, even here with me.' But his shirt smelled like hammered flax, the honeybee.

"I wanted him to touch me. I wanted him to give me a new way of thinking.

"'You'll be safe there,' he told me at the end of lunch, pointing to these leaves. 'Things are going to get worse for me.' That made me angry. This tree, this shadow of the leaf across my foot, my hand on the bark.

"The skin on the backsides of his hands was unusual. And a crack ran through his front tooth. He touched it often with his tongue, telling me a boy hit him in the mouth with a stick. 'Did I tell you the story of that boy?' he asked as if we'd been friends a long while. He seemed to have his eye out for that kid, looking away from me several times that afternoon. At the wall, the gate.

"Salt crusts my eyes. I unwrapped his picture and leaned it against this branch. He stood with his foot on the ledge of my pool when I snapped it. He was smiling, can you see? We'd just gotten back. This picture frame casts a sharp shadow so I use it as a clock. His face inside the frame against the branch. I mark my days this way, dividing them into morning and evening, dividing them into hours.

"At night when I fold my sash in front of his picture I think, if I could become a man entirely without purpose I could forget him completely. But even now when I say the word 'purposeless' my body springs up to resist it. So you see I have my job cut out.

"Sometimes I say to myself, or to the spider in the cracks of the bark, to the ants, the webbing, I say, 'It never happened.' And if I could persuade myself of this, even if only for a few hours, I could begin to say, 'I have no hunger, I have no thirst.' But his voice was a low tenor when he sang and he only sang when we walked in my garden. So it's impossible for me. 'I feel at home here,' he said, gesturing to my vines.

"This rust-brown water in my cupped hands. Nothing special.

"When he touched my shoulder something covered me like a film. It was a feeling, a sensation. I think I felt pure-hearted.

"When I scrambled down to show him the way to my house I snagged the toe of my silk slipper. Women laughed at me. The men grabbed the coin purses inside their trousers. I think they worried I'd cheat them again right there, in front of him. At the time, they disgusted me. But now, my toes are covered with black hairs and you can see my feet are like a monkey's. Now I run along these branches watching for his return. I've hung no mirrors. The light turns everything blue. The cart in the far field. The hills that rob the horizon of its purity.

"Mira set out the sweet dates that afternoon, the wine. She hurried to have things ready. I paid her double. We weren't accustomed to having houseguests. She made me look good. Kind and generous. I tipped her in front of him so he would see my generosity. His hand on my cheek, his voice that found me behind my mask of leaves.

"The commerce of these leaves I break against my skin, the sharp edges cutting in, the pungent smell. I hold them in my palms this way to find him but he isn't here. Sometimes the fragrance takes me to a palace of memory. The corridors are cool and marble. I climb in to find him. A chair, a throne where he should sit, empty, its eagle's wings carved and gilded. Once I thought I saw him crouching there behind it, his hands covering his head, the blue band of a silver robe fell around him like a lake. But the image disappeared.

"They ransacked my house. One found the bolt of red silk hidden under my bed, another, my good oil, the dipping spoon, my favorite pillow embroidered with beads. I should have given him the beaded pillow. Feathers flew everywhere. My favorite dresser thrown against this trunk, its delicate inlaid bands of ivory like the fingers of a wife I never had, white and candle-slender, the elongated joints.

"One by one they hurled what they'd taken against the trunk of this tree, yelling epithets. Their anger was like fire. I thought they'd put a torch to this trunk and burn me like a spit goat. But I was lucky. Their voices were truthful. I am not a good man.

"I was angry. I'd already repaid them double but it didn't matter. My silk pillow filled with lavender. I said, 'Go ahead! Take it, you lousy bastards!' The drawers of the dresser fallen out on each other like stairs, the veneer peeled away. The thin bands of ivory, pried out and stolen. The jar broken, the sweet oil dripping down the dresser, precious oil cured by the sun, dried to a black mark.

My silk robe, flung open, ripped. My home is occupied by rats now. I see them come and go.

"A man's voice came up through the branches. It was a Friday. His voice was like a crow caw, jeering. 'Zaccheus, they killed your hero!' He threw sand up at me then ran. I wept but I didn't believe him. That was twenty-seven years ago and thirty-two days. This blue light, his hand on the table, his voice in the wind. I keep a jar of water for him, even though he doesn't come. Sometimes I call him 'The visitor who doesn't come.'

"Every Friday I bind my head with thin branches to honor that rumor, even though I refuse to believe it. I bind my head on Fridays to tell myself the rumor isn't true. To say the one I love will come back to me. Come back to this tree. I can picture him clearly, walking toward me on stones of forgiveness.

"Today is the Sabbath. My early days here, a young girl came from Jericho with her widowed mother to cultivate balsam, which they sold in the marketplace. Sticky and resinous, used as a medicine and in making perfume. I knew that much. But the young girl said, 'It mitigates suffering,' which caught my attention. When she said balsam is also used to embalm the dead, I grew quiet.

"The first time, she tied food in a scarf and raised it into my branches by a rope: palm cake, coconut butter, skewered bits of lamb, a small grilled fish, dried peas. 'Go away!' I yelled down at her. 'Never come back!' The next time, three dates in a muslin bag. They dangled in the air for weeks. Her kindness was unbearable. I buried the sweet things up high in the trunk.

"Then she put a flask of water to the end of the rope. I threw it down so it crashed against the ground. Then she went to the river for brackish water. Between the reeds, the green moss floating the way it does, on the surface. 'It's unclean,' she called up to me, so I took it, jerking the jug up quickly and disappearing with it into my leaves.

"The next day I saw her approaching from a distance. She balanced her weight on the dresser drawers, with a hot bowl of lentils and coriander, holding it level as she climbed. 'Hello,' she said and I moved downward, toward her. 'I see you behind those leaves.' Hunched in the crook of the tree, her bowl of lentils against my bruised and hairy knees. I'd come down from the high branches.

"She gave me lentils in a bowl. Her mother warned her that I was hated and dangerous, but she visited me anyway. 'He's an animal, don't take so much,' she waved her spoon in the air over the pot. 'Let him stay in that tree forever, like a prison.' When she told me this I felt a blankness between them where love could have been. On her sleeve there was a leaf pattern, the beads from my embroidered pillow sewn there. I wondered if she knew where the beads came from.

"Eventually, I moved further out to another sycamore. Past Jericho, past Joshua's horn. I soaked palm leaves, wove them into mats, offered them to visitors. It was a new generation. People came. I didn't know what they wanted. It perplexed me at first. They built hermitages. One planted an herb garden with stakes and string. They called their gathering Cellia, the cells. Called themselves monks. One told me they numbered over two hundred, circling my tree. Then there were more. Some stayed a few days, some never left. 'But what's here?' I ask myself. Mats. Leaves. Memories. Emptiness.

"The heart hungers for what is absolute, for a cause worthy of itself, and actual. You know this, Mary of Magdala. Christ on the throne, those Byzantine eyes. I've heard how they follow you around a room. That's what we want, isn't it? To be seen. That's what I tell them. My fingers drag a small wake in the dust on this leaf.

"Sometimes I yell at the monks, 'What was the color of his hair? Tell me the color of his hair! I'm forgetting!' I scream down at them and they fall silent, pity on their faces. But they didn't know him. Most of them were too young. Forced to live on stories of him as if it were bread. It's not the same. This tree emptied of sap, only the fibrous wood of the hours, one after the other and no shape to them. I'm on the lookout just to keep myself from bitterness.

"I have my knife and pen and kite. This small gold bowl. This ring. The water in the marsh will turn blue again. My memory of him, the everlasting sun.

"I think of that young girl and her mother. I don't know what happened to them. One night in my imagination I traveled to find her, to find what was good between them. I went for the young girl's sake."

THE REST OF the story was told in the Annals of the community, which Mary later read. The record indicated this:

ZACCHEUS CRIED FOR the young girl and her mother. He cried for himself and those he robbed. Most of all he cried for the One who didn't come back, the One he looked for in the breaking of the leaves. He cried all night. Contrition ran down the bark, stripping away the leaves. Salt joined salt. Sorrow in the gashes.

IN THE MORNING, after his night of weeping, a new monk brought Zaccheus food. Expecting to raise it on a rope thrown over the branches, he found the tree bare of leaves.

"Holy Father, Zaccheus!" he called out. When there was no answer, he ventured to the first branch, the second. Found Zaccheus resting high in the crook of the tree. His arms and legs were folded up against his narrow chest, his grey beard stiff, his skin dry, his fingers clamped around a jar of fresh water, a wreath of leaves on his head. Putting his ear to the chest and then the mouth, confirming what he feared, the new monk scrambled down, ran back to his cell, returned with a bolt of red silk, dusty and fraying.

At the same time, the young girl, now married and with children of her own, sat counting the week's earnings. Her reputation for balsam had grown so that she'd made her husband wealthy and her three sons. Setting coin on top of coin she stopped suddenly, her fingers draping the pile of coins, her mind caught in a day vision of a man crouching behind a throne, wearing a silver robe with blue banding. Leaving the counting table she walked past the river to the sycamore tree where he used to live, seeing, again, the heap of broken things, jagged bits of wood, clay, tattered silks. Her youngest son on her hip, she noted that it was his hunger for righteousness that drew her to him. The hunger to change his life. She had the same hunger. This is a day of turning, she told herself. If I cleave, cleave.

HEARING THE NEWS, two thousand monks gathered at the base of the sycamore tree. Carefully they lifted Zaccheus down, wrapped his body in the red cloth. Buried him, with the jug of water, in the new church, beside the high altar.

Among themselves the monks spoke of the purity of his heart. They elected him one of the original twelve, replacing Judas Iscariot. After a period of mourning, they opened the large book and entered the day of his death, listing it as his birth date, to be observed like the feast day of a saint. They spoke of his confidence that the Messiah would return, while noting that he never used the word "Messiah" or any other title, but spoke only of the visitor, using tender nicknames, if he spoke at all.

That night all two thousand monks had the same dream. They learned this the next morning, comparing notes. The details varied somewhat, but each found himself standing in a long marble corridor, a palace of memory, where there was, in the distance, an empty throne. They saw Father Zaccheus crouching behind it in a silver robe, the blue trim of the garment spread around him like a lake.

43

John on Patmos

E XILED, NO ONE to talk to, no one to listen, his hair in knots, infested with lice, John cast out his net of words, hoping to catch himself like a fish.

Touching the trunk of a palm, its segmented layers like playing cards but rough against his hands, he whispered, "Wasn't I the one he loved? Wasn't I the one who rested on his breast?"

The trunk mute, the fronds silent above. He poked a sea anemone with a stick. "You there! Speak up. That last night with the tearing of the bread, didn't he say he loved me?" The anemone closed in, withdrawing its soft, mushy green.

Each night he recited a litany to the fire. "I, John, was there when he raised Jairus's daughter from the dead. I was there on the holy mountain when he became like light. Peter and James were with me. They are my witnesses. They would say, 'It happened.' And I was the one he loved."

When the driftwood turned from red to white he told himself, "This is corroboration."

He did not take shelter from the sun. His eyebrows whitened. His lashes grew thick and interwoven. His skin gathered to itself a calcium casing of sea salts. Sand crabs made their home on the top sides of his feet. His hair grew long, he wrapped it around his waist like a belt.

After one hundred days he no longer remembered the house of Jairus. Or Moses and Elijah on the holy mountain, how they stood in the flagrant light. Instead he heard tambourines and the small sound of finger drums in the night. Trumpets. He saw stars falling like candlesticks. He dreamt of locusts shaped like horses, wearing crowns of gold, their tails like scorpions with deadly sting.

He heard strange words, Gog and Magog, in his sleep. Waking he thought, now it is happening. I am going mad.

He called the sand "Whoremonger!" The sea anemone "Sorcerer!" He cursed them all into a lake of fire. He no longer wanted someone to say, "It happened, John. Jairus, the holy mountain, leaning on his breast. It is your history. It all belongs to you."

Instead he told himself, "I am a sea urchin with purple spines. I have no memory, no feelings, no thought at all."

Still the visions came.

An earth scorched by fire. Sea, black as sackcloth. The moon, blood. He cursed memory, called it the "Mother of Harlots," "Babylon." He sat as still as stone. Told himself, "I am no longer a sea urchin with purple spines. I am not here at all."

A SILVER FISH landed on the shore. Large, like none he'd seen before. He smelled it and thought, the pelican must have left this for me. Even though he had never seen the pelican. He did not eat the fish. He refused to believe in miracles.

He felt a pecking on his cheek. With his fingers, he pulled apart his lids. Salt crumbled in his fingertips. On his shoulder, a black crow sat with its narrow yellow beak. He knew it was not an island bird.

He heard voices. Soldiers lifted him to their boat. They said, "We have a new Emperor. Your exile is revoked."

IN THE ROCKING of the boat he heard the voice of the one he once loved, saying, "John, I come quickly!" In the sky he saw a woman clothed with the sun.

He saw the distant coastline, white roofs of houses, and thought, they are taking me to the Holy City. I see its foundation laid with jasper and chalcedony. He called to the soldiers, "Look! We are going to Paradise!"

JOHN'S WORDS CROSSED the Aegean.

New Christians found themselves caught in his net.

So many silver fish, they canonized him.

They didn't call him John the Raving or John the Lunatic.

They called him John the Theologian, John the Divine.

They gathered his nightmares into a book and called it *Revelation*.

44

Mary the Mother of Jesus, Later in Life

A S SHE AGED and death approached, Mary tried to read the book of her life.

In silence and modesty, in the absence of things most powerful.

She had intended to paint the glorious mysteries of her son's life. When he walked on water, when he left the tomb, when he appeared to the disciples on the shore after his death. To paint him in his glory and around him scenes of his life, but instead she painted humbler ones. When Joseph lifted her onto the donkey. When they stopped for shade and he brought grapes from a basket, when they ate together under a tree, gathering wildflowers and berries. Joseph in his first workshop building a large table they never used. The birthday party when he reminded her they were a holy family. She painted her husband at Golgatha, even though she hadn't seen him there and had heard nothing from him in years. And on his head, she painted a nimbus.

What survives? she wondered. Love and the memory of grapes.

45

Joseph the Dreamer

JOSEPH SAW THE followers of his son increase rapidly and dreamt that they would continue to increase until time came to an end. He saw that experience would be put into words and heard a creed that was starting to form, followers calling Jesus, "God from God, Light from Light, begotten not made, one in being the Father."

He lay in his room, just his donkey outside in the courtyard, the arbor with its dormant vine. It seemed he was dying, but he wasn't quite sure. Though he still didn't want them, dreams came, and he remembered his cousins saying when he was young, "Here comes the dreamer!"

Sliding in and out of sleep, he saw a future in which some men and women would be reverenced after their deaths like his son already was, and some would be given patronages. He, too, would become such a patron, attached to the well-being of cabinetmakers, carpenters, confectioners, dying people, and engineers. But he would also be the patron saint "against doubt," which saddened him.

Some would believe that he and Mary never married but remained betrothed only. Some, that he was old when they met, she a child and he a mere guardian. For many, that they had never had sex, much less enjoyed and then missed it, a castrating thought. Worst, to a few, he would be seen as a willing cuckold, letting others devotedly love his wife more intimately than he had and this hurt the most.

It was all awkward like so much else had been. Stepping off a cliff into the still, dark night.

"No one will quote me," he told himself when the mood came most heavily, seeing again that everything rolled out toward another glory.

And it was true. He would nowhere be quoted in the scriptures Christians collected and formalized, and would not be the object of any special devotion for more than one thousand years.

Outside, the finches and hollyhocks.

MOVING IN AND out of visions and dreams, he saw an ornate city with a central square guarded by a quadragga of life-sized gilded bronze horses. Orphans and unwanted babies were placed in baskets and left there in the portico of a hospital run by nuns who fed, clothed and educated them as they grew. The girls were taught music, the boys trades and the hospital treated people with syphilis and other incurable diseases, the church being named the Incurabili. Joseph liked that odd combination of syphilis, orphans and polyphonic music. That there was compassion where there was little hope. He liked that the church was modest and well-made.

He thought of the Slain Infants, that night that still cut like a ravine, and saw that the church of his son was built on pain that was ancient, unchanging, and inescapable. He recalled that Mary told him she was feeling this when Jesus was just an infant and he regretted having dismissed her at the time, because she was right.

The older he became, the less he understood. The old drawings of the bull tacked to the wall, those years when he hoped to understand his life by simplifying it, were ragged and yellow with age.

He wondered if any of the brothers or sisters of those who were slain became followers of his son. He wondered if any of the Incurabili orphans did. How would faith be possible for them? He had no answer. A breeze through the window, another drawing fell to the floor, and he realized he was an expert in doubt after all.

What he did know, however, he would tell anyone who asked. He would say that there is loneliness in doubting because doubt misses its twin, which is wonder. And there is loneliness in skepticism because it misses its twin, which is awe.

The Angelus sounded in the clay bell down the street.

"Come, my good Master," the donkey said. "I am taking you to glory."

46

The Dormition of the Virgin

M ARY LAY ON a litter surrounded by people she knew and loved, some having come from great distances, Rome, Macedonia and Greece.

She heard them whispering phrases to each other, giving her titles, the words afloat in the air above her bed, "Anchor," "Mother of Sorrows," "Our Lady of the Sign." But she said to herself, "I am a bulrush that grew in the mud. I'm neither Moses nor Pharaoh. I am the wet, muddy reed." Had she the energy, she might have corrected them, saying, "Call me 'Mary of the Bulrushes,' 'The Woven Cradle,' 'Mother of the Grassy Marsh.'"

SHE'D WONDERED SINCE she first heard the words, what it meant to be "blessed among women" and had performed an examination since she was young. She'd wanted to say then, "O yes, this is who I am, blessed among women." But she could not say those words either then or now. As a girl she'd had her childish ways. She'd engaged in small deceptions, had been sarcastic at times and

impatient, which she'd worked on with modest success when she
first met Joseph. And she'd regularly neglected the sick.

SHE COULD HEAR them starting to pray, heard the sound of bread
being set down on a plate, a cup being filled with wine. They were
gathering around her table, the sound of their feet on the floor,
slow motion, bodies adjusting to her small space, fabric touching
fabric, that hush, a cough, the words murmured quietly in unison,
words of consecration and remembrance, and she hungered with a
heated, impatient desire to see her son again face to face. She knew
that it was the magnitude of God's intention in his son, through
her, that made her unlike other women, made her graced condition
so full and nothing else.

WHEN THEY WERE finished, and the silence that followed also
reached its end, she heard more titles, "She Who Shows the Way,"
"Throne of Wisdom." She turned her head toward the window.
The words now seemed to come from outside, from beyond her
room, from beyond the tree and garden wall. She didn't under-
stand all of them. "Mother of the Poor," "Joy of the Just," "Our
Lady of Lebanon," and then from across the sea, "Our Lady of
Mt. Carmel," "Notre Dame." In the high mountains, "Ark of the
Covenant," "Tower of David," "Queen of Peace."

　　She felt as she had when she was fifteen and Joseph a year older
and the machinery working through their lives had no precedent.
They will make their own versions of me, putting themselves here,
she realized, it is happening already. She again felt that she should

surrender. She didn't hear, "Mother of the Bulrushes" and "Mary of Wet Feet," she heard, "Theotokos" and "Mother of God."

She should surrender so others could make of her life what they needed to make. Hadn't the bulrushes consented to not only preserve Moses but also to be home to tadpoles and small fishes, while to the egrets and plovers, a hunting ground?

THEY WERE COMING back to her bed now, some weeping, some touching her feet through the blanket. She saw that she would be both glorious and, to others, to most, nameless.

The candles were burning.

Where is the holy?

SHE SAW THE future as if it were already past and watched as a woman took two palm fronds and folded them to make a cross. It was Palm Sunday. Leaving Church, she took the cross home and fastened it to a plaster figure she called "The Blessed Virgin" that stood in the corner of her front yard. Chain-link fence, pick-up trucks, the statue in a blue robe. Over the statue, the woman had propped an umbrella for protection against rain and to the scalloped edge of the umbrella she'd attached a string of Christmas lights.

Easter and Christmas, umbrellas and folded palms and blood and trucks and water and cement and plaster and grass and chain link all assembled into a web of meaning, into a world. Lawn chairs, a planter made of stacked rubber tires, a watch dog, a torn couch, all of it a hymn.

Holding fast to the particular, Mary thought, as energy seeped from her body, this great hymn of the ordinary is what God needs. This is what he has always needed. And with that, angels and seraphim with six wings, she projected forward and stepped out of time.

47

Jonah in the 21st Century

S OMETIMES HE STILL feels revulsion toward himself like he
did in the days of Nineveh. At worst, it comes like an affliction that staggers him, washing over with such force that he has to
hold on to the wall or the arm of a chair to steady himself, sometimes the arm of a stranger. "I am a man with an ice cream cone!"
he said out loud just yesterday. "I am just a man with an ice cream
cone!" But it slayed him nonetheless.

When it passed and he'd finished his ice cream and almost felt
calm again, though exhausted, he remembered the mariners who,
despite their distress and terror, did not want to cast him into the
sea, but rowed valiantly trying to reach shore. He wanted to be
like them then and wants to be like them now. Their smooth, blue
features, their clear vision and simple hats.

IT WAS A relief when God let him go and Jonah stepped out of his
diamond suit. His wife and child, both happy to have him back,

loved him so ardently that on some days he actually felt worthy of their love, felt almost like those sailors, even though they had their gods and he no longer had his. Sometimes he would tell his wife, "I really am a sailor!" and dance with her around the room. He feels it even when his affliction comes, now, two thousand years later, and feels it this afternoon as he sits in a room hearing confessions offered by the faithful.

THE SECOND TEENAGE boy has left the confessional and wakes a woman asleep on her chair. When she stands, he holds the door slightly open for her, which surprises her, so kind and unexpected. She begins in an uncustomary way.

"You might have to help me do this," she clears her throat. "I don't remember all of the words. It's been more than thirty years since my last confession."

Inside, in the dark pocket, they see each other through the screen. She lowers herself to the worn wood kneeler and sees that what was once three compartments is now all one small room with a narrow passage by which she could step around the screen and speak to the priest directly. To do that, she would have to stoop slightly and walk a few steps to where he sits quietly on a very low stool, vested and still. She feels his deep regard for her, startling in its sweetness, so that she stays composed but only with effort. The dark wood lit by a short candle on a table next to his stool. Like being in the body of a great fish, she thinks, the church its sea and beyond that, the vast sea.

SHE DIDN'T EXPECT to cry when she volunteers that she has been all these years in an argument with God because he let things happen that never should have happened.

"I want to believe that he loves the world. And I want to believe," here she suddenly can't continue, which she also did not expect, as she'd rehearsed this in the cab hoping to be concise, which is not her strong suit. She wipes her cheeks, which are wet now, because she has come to the center of things. "I want to believe that he loves even me."

SOMETIMES THE SIDE of his face is to the screen, his eyes closed, his hand holding his chin, and sometimes he turns and looks directly at her and she looks at him. The stool is so low that when they do look at each other, even though she is kneeling, he is still below her slightly so that he looks up to her, which feels intentional and respectful, that he is perhaps there in the service of one thing, which is mercy.

She could live here, she decides, for the rest of her life. Close to everything important, but hidden. She hears the heartbeat in the fleshy walls.

He waits until she has finished and finds he empathizes with the woman on the other side of the screen.

"I don't feel I'm committing a sin that I can't believe in God anymore. I can't will it. What happened, happened. But I really wish it would change. This is why I came." She wants her integrity and her faith, both at the same time, and Jonah smiles, the breathing of the whale, the constant flow of water around his face and body, water in and out through the baleen, seaweed tangled in his hair. He wonders if, on one day at one hour, she yelled the same thing at God, "Let me go! I'm no longer your prophet! I want to be a sailor."

"It's not a sin to refuse to believe in a God who's too small," he replies and his certainty touches her. "To doubt the God you believe in is to serve him. It's an offering. It's your gift."

SHE KNOWS PEOPLE are waiting on the cool, hard chairs but she does not want to leave.

"Are you sorry for your sins?" he asks with a clean directness that brings her back to the matter at hand. She sees sorrow is what now matters to him and she remembers that it is part of the formulary. That he has to ask her this, the hinge on which the sacrament rests. She is sorry for her fear and how it leads to other things in her life that she regrets, impatience, lack of kindness, judging others, and so she says truthfully, "Yes."

He recites the words of absolution with an ancient authority that comes to her through his thick Filipino accent, his extremely soft voice. He speaks the words of absolution on behalf of the God she cannot see and cannot believe in as she once had. Standing, his palm raised, through the screen, the ancient words come over her like water, "God the Father of mercies, through the death and resurrection of his Son has reconciled the world to himself and sent the Holy Spirit among us for the forgiveness of sins; through the ministry of the Church may God give you pardon and peace, and

I absolve you from your sins in the name of the Father, and of the Son, and of the Holy Spirit."

"Amen" she says, crossing herself.

"I'm glad you came," he tells her. "Do you know the Hail Mary?" She answers that she does know it. "Say it once, slowly, and receive your forgiveness. If you commit a mortal sin," he says and this shocks her, thinking murder, theft, adultery, "come sooner. Otherwise, try to go to mass every Sunday and come back to confession in three months. This is April. So come back in July. Can you do that? Three months, not thirty years," again, he smiles.

WHEN EVERYONE HAS come and gone and dusk settles on the roof of the church and the rectory, he emerges through the narrow door, which each person also entered. In the sacristy he removes his vestments, kisses the altar and retires to his small apartment at the rear of the property.

Just inside his front door hangs the first of a series of nautical maps that circle the walls. On the kitchen table, by the toaster, a small collection of maritime paraphernalia that he likes to hold until they warm in his hands, a compact telescope, a brass pulley, a short piece of rope he ties into maritime knots, halyard hitch and cat's paw, doing it absentmindedly the way another person might handle prayer beads, waiting as the water heats on the stove. On the coffee table, next to his Bible and crucifix, a small scrimshaw carved on whalebone shows the image of a sailor. Made in the nineteenth century, the sailor wears a striped shirt, a necktie, and a neat jacket with buttons. He is surrounded by a wreath of leaves and under the wreath an anchor. Since it was carved before 1973, he reminds himself, whenever his eye falls upon it, that it is legal for him to possess it, which is important as he thinks of himself as a simple, law-abiding priest.

THE WOMAN LOOKED up at the high dome before leaving, having said one Hail Mary thoughtfully while kneeling on a pew. She didn't show the priest her book, hadn't even thought of it, and put it inside her purse. Come back in three months to see if I've improved, she writes on a small paper, like a doctor's appointment, and then the priest's final words, which were, "Be happy! It's Easter!" even though today is Good Friday, which surprised her again. Good Friday, when all the evidence of God's presence is removed. The day of God's complete abasement. Not Easter, the day Christ was risen, but the day he was crucified. But this also seems fitting and true. That something good would come from the future, and that it already has, wrapping itself around her, radiating backward three days from Sunday to where she now stands, at the bus stop, squinting into the sun.

Notes

I.

Cain and the Dream of the City | words of the snow king are here adapted from the oldest known Scandinavian hymn, composed in the 13th Century by the Icelandic chieftain Kolbeinn Tumason, purportedly written on his deathbed. Music was composed 700 years later by Thorkell Sigurbjörnsson. Performed with full English translation at www.onbeing.org/blog/an-icelandic -hymn-transports-us-all-video/6746.

Isaac in the Field | the phrase "protecting veil" from "The Protecting Veil (for Cello and String Orchestra)" by John Tavener. Sony Classical Recording.

Moses and the Burning Bush | *Miserere mei, Deus, secundum magnam misericordiam tuam* (Pity me, O God, according to Thy great mercy), words of the Latin antiphon said or sung at a Roman

Catholic Solemn Mass in all liturgical seasons except the Easter season and Palm Sunday, based on Psalm 51. Set to music by Allegri and gorgeously performed by the Choir of New College, Oxford at www.youtube.com/watch?v=36Y_ztEW1NE.

The Queen of Sheba | here attributed to the "voice of reason" heard by the Queen of Sheba are lines taken from the Hungaroton CD "Magyar Gregoriánum, 2, Gregorian Chants from Medieval Hungary, Advent, Christmas, Pentecost," performed in Latin by Schola Hungarica, 1978, particularly the hymns "Ecce carissimi" (Lo, my dear ones) and "Alleluia."

Jonah | "basilica of bones" adapted from the line, "Amid the ducts, inside the basilica of bones," by Jack Gilbert in *Refusing Heaven*. New York: Alfred A. Knopf, 2005.

II.

The Annunciation | Adapted with permission from *The Memory Room*. Washington, DC: Counterpoint Press, 2002.

The Visitation | "hail of stones"—see *The Guardian*, online edition, Thursday, 8 July 2010. For 21st-Century human rights violations, death by stoning, see www.richarddawkins.net/news _articles/2013.

Joseph's Decision | the title "Queen of Galilee" from "The Cherry-Tree Carol," a Christmas folk song sung since the 15th Century, the story derived from the apocryphal *Gospel of Pseudo-Matthew* written c. 600–625 AD. Of the many current recordings see www.youtube.com/watch?v=H5DSEeqnwjE or www.youtube .com/watch?v=HOTM_ZLPfDM.

The Nativity of Jesus | for the doubt of Joseph see "The Nativity of Christ" in *The Meaning of Icons* by Leonid Ouspensky and Vladimir Lossky. Crestwood, New York: St. Vladimir's Seminary Press, 1982; for "the transparent structure of the world" see Henri Cole's poem "Gulls" in *Blackbird and Wolf*. New York: Farrar, Straus and Giroux , 2007.

Mary Loving-kindness | for "understanding things about which I have no empirical knowledge," see Henri Cole's poem "Birthday" in *Blackbird and Wolf*; for the incurability of suffering see "Icons of Loving-kindness" in *The Meaning of Icons*.

The Murder of Zachariah | see "Elizabeth and the Infant on Seeking Refuge in the Mountain from the Pursuing Soldier," *Yaroslavian Icon Painting*, by S. I. Maslenitsyn. Moscow: Iskusstvo Publishers, 1983.

Elizabeth | the "elongated face indicating a preacher of penitence," see "St. John the Forerunner" in *The Meaning of Icons*.

John the Forerunner in the Wilderness | see "Scenes from the Life of John the Baptist in the Wilderness," *Yaroslavian Icon Painting.*

Legion | ". . . love is punctured" is a variation on "Plato, for whom love has not been punctured," Henri Cole, "Birthday" in *Blackbird and Wolf.* Also from Cole, "Today is flaring up" is a variation on ". . . Wednesday is flaring up" in "The Erasers" in *Blackbird and Wolf.* "I see a bloodstained toad instead of my white kitten," from Cole's "The Tree Cutters," also in *Blackbird and Wolf.*

Veronica | Reprinted with permission from *The Memory Room.*

Mary Magdalen at Golgatha | "But, Mary, look at me and see. It isn't true that you were never loved," adapted from Cole, "It is not true, after all, that you were never loved" in "Self-Portrait with Red Eyes," *Blackbird and Wolf.*

God | "Take him, he's yours," adapted from "'Oh, let him be,' God is saying, 'I made him,'" in Cole's poem "Dune," *Blackbird and Wolf.*

Joseph of Arimathea | "chaos of mercy and the swiftness of revenge," adapted from "the chaos of revenge and the smooth order of forgiveness" in Cole's "Persimmon Tree" in *Blackbird and Wolf.*

Zaccheus | see Gimpei's disdain for his feet, his body like a monkey, in Yusunari Kawabata's *The Lake*. Tokyo: Kodansha International Ltd., 1974.

John on Patmos | reprinted with permission from *The Memory Room*.

The Dormition of the Virgin | tradition concerning the last days and death of the Virgin Mary is based on the teachings of Dionysius the Aeropagite (d. 107 AD), first Bishop of Athens later quoted by Ambrose of Milan (d. 397 AD) in *On Virginity*. See www.pravo-slavie.ru/english/48309.htm. For the hymn of the ordinary, see also Jack Gilbert, "What we feel most has no name but amber, archers, cinnamon, horses, and birds," in "The Forgotten Dialect of the Heart," in *The Great Fires: Poems, 1982-1992*. New York: Alfred A. Knopf, 1994.

Jonah in the 21st Century | "To doubt the God you believe in is to serve him," Christopher Bollen speaking with Joshua Ferris about *To Rise Again at a Decent Hour* in *Interview* magazine, May 2014.

Acknowledgments

THE JOYFUL, IMPOSSIBLE task. But to begin. I am grateful for,

scientists and rationalists of all persuasions who push outward our understanding of the real world and to those who, by their example, show that it is more honorable to abandon an idea of god that is too small than to honor it;

Sunday School teachers of all times and circumstances who fearlessly take upon themselves the task of introducing to three-year-olds the most ambitious literary text of Western Civilization;

members of cloistered communities in all faiths who rise in the dark of night to pray for the brokenness of the world while the rest of us sleep;

designers, architects, composers and artists of all kinds who, through their work, bring into the physical world what at first they alone could see, making our world more dense with meaning, more transparent and more deeply human;

my children and children by marriage, Augie, Joey, Madeline, Ikuko, Rana and Roman, through whom I learn that unconditional love is not only a noble idea but is also real, abundant and free; and to my five grandchildren who, though very young, ask ethical and religious questions of their own accord, reminding me that to be human is to be unlike every other living thing;

friends who keep me on the high ground from which all good work comes: Jeremy Foss, Arch Getty, Leo Harrington, Enrique Martinéz Celaya, Jim and Jane Sherry, Scott and Jeannie Wood; and to writer friends, Julianne Cohen, Sam Dunn, Janet Fitch, Jody Hauber, Ilya Kaminsky, Rochelle Low and Rita Williams who read the early work and refused to commend it when it was horrid yet pointed me toward what might be good—for their candor and kindness. And particularly to David Francis and Garth Greenwell who, over years, turned from their own splendid work to give extraordinary attentiveness to mine;

Whale & Star and Lannan Foundation, particularly Jo Chapman, for giving me a generous Literary Fellowship and writing residencies without asking anything in return and without receiving anything for many years, thus showing me what patience and faith in another person looks like;

LaunchPodium, particularly Bridie and Mike Parsons, Robert Shabazz and Marielle Sedin who energetically brought their expertise to my world, extending the reach of this text into the ever-changing digital environment; and to Radu Cautis who first conceived of this and helped put it into motion;

and for Counterpoint Press, Rolph Blythe, Megan Fishmann, Matthew Hoover, Megan Jones, Corinne Kalasky, Claire Shalinsky, Diane Turso, Charlie Winton, Sharon Wu and the entire crew who gave this new text its home. And most particularly for Jack Shoemaker, who kept and keeps *The Memory Room* in print for 13 years without earning a dime, silently and staunchly maintaining in his person a barrier between art and the bottom line, thus providing writers with that perfect and priceless habitat in which to feel meaningless, to graze, to rise up and then to run.